THE WORD ON THE STREET

"*Kai'Ro* is a must read for urban youth and youth workers. This book is destined to become a classic. Judah Ben has wonderfully captured the journey of an urban Pilgrim navigating the pitfalls of life through God's presence."

Dana L. Thomas
Executive Director // Kids Across America // Branson, Missouri

"My teenage son read *Kai'Ro* along with me and found it to be just as enticing as I did. He then read it again and again. This is the reaction from someone who does not enjoy reading. *Kai'Ro* has been an excellent discipleship tool for my son to share with his friends and other youth groups."

Tonya Jones
Mother and Urban Youth Worker // Birmingham, AL

"Judah Ben does a masterful job of taking a classic 300 year old Christian allegory and making it palatable for 21st century urban taste buds. The characters and settings of *Kai'Ro* are relevant, the plot is compelling, and the Gospel is strikingly clear. Urban themes and vices are woven into the mix with great care and precision, offering a vision of the Gospel of the glory of Christ that has the power to have urban youth on a reckless pursuit for the all satisfying God. The final allegory, climax, and resolution are gripping as he parts ways with Bunyan to give the reader much to chew on in the end. If urban youth get a hold of the Bible-centered gems found in this book, the inner-city will never be the same again. I pray, Oh God, that you would make it so!"

Raymond Causly II
Church Planter // Compton, California

"Outside of the Bible, this is my favorite book I have ever taught in the classroom. *Kai'Ro* is chalked full of modern-day experiences and language that teens can relate to and countless teachable moments for instructors to use. I find my students continually reading ahead to see what happens, and in today's culture you will not find too many books that spark that kind of curiosity. I would highly recommend this book to any one teaching young people in our American culture."

High School Teacher // Restoratio

D1519206

"I found *Kai'Ro* to be a compelling, creative, and realistic portrayal of the challenges, responsibilities, sacrifices, and joys that come with living for Jesus Christ...it is a great evangelistic and discipleship tool to use in prison ministry, which is what we are all about at Prison Fellowship."

Becky Beane
Senior Editor, Corporate Communications // Prison Fellowship

"Something old - something new! This provocative work is a re-presentation of John Bunyan's, *The Pilgrim's Progress*, expressing its allegorical truths in fresh, new ways, speaking in the idiom of a youth culture which desperately needs to be initiated into the faith, instructed about the faith and inspired to keep the faith. *Kai'Ro* possesses the potential of being an instrument which can bridge the gap between races. It is a book that must be viewed through fresh eyes and given a new hearing."

Robert Smith, Jr.
Professor and Author // Beeson Divinity School // Birmingham, Alabama

"We've all heard the phrase, 'Think outside the box,' to think differently, unconventionally, or from a new perspective. That's exactly what Judah Ben has done in writing *Kai'Ro*, using characters, challenges and lingo that the contemporary urban reader will readily identify with. Youth workers, parents, and teachers alike will find *Kai'Ro* a valuable resource in discipling the minds of urban youth."

Ron Carter
Director of Training and Resources
The DeVos Urban Leadership Initiative // Grand Rapids, Michigan

"This work challenges us in a uniquely creative way to examine our identity and our purpose. It provides real hope—a real destination—for those who have felt unsure along life's journey. I especially recommend *Kai'Ro* to those working with young people, particularly in poverty stricken areas. A spiritual jolt for some, an awakening for others, *Kai'Ro* has awesome evangelistic possibilities."

Carolyn Maull McKinstry
President // Sixteenth Street Foundation, Inc. // Birmingham, Alabama

"KAI-RO"

THE JOURNEY OF AN URBAN PILGRIM
by JUDAH BEN

KAI-RO PROJECT

HANDS of HUR

Kai'Ro: The Journey of an Urban Pilgrim
by Judah Ben

Printed in China

ISBN: 978 0 615 32721 1

5 6 7 8 9 / 15 14 13 12

*Cover and interior design by **geoff sciacca design***

To my students at Restoration Academy. May you find and keep to the little dirt road that lies just beyond the hedges.

ABOUT THE AUTHOR:

Judah Ben, mid-30s, has been involved with urban youth since his family moved to Birmingham, Alabama in the early '90s. His vision for urban ministry was birthed while working on his undergraduate degree at Wheaton College. For over two years he met weekly with youth incarcerated in the Cook County Juvenile Detention Center in Chicago. Upon graduating in 2000, he returned home to teach at Restoration Academy, a young, urban Christian School in Fairfield, Alabama seeking to rescue youth from the lure of the streets. The school has since become a place where strong academics, competitive athletics, and a caring Christian faculty empower students to graduate from high school, attend college, and begin a life of hope and promise. Judah Ben earned a Masters Degree at Covenant College and is now an administrator at Restoration Academy. He and his wife and four children make their home in the neighborhood.

The Kai'Ro Project is an urban resource initiative offering biblically-based discipleship materials to those involved in urban ministry. The books, *Kai'Ro: The Journey of an Urban Pilgrim*, and *Kai'Ro: the Homecoming* are the core. Leaders' Guides for both books have also been developed and are available on the Project website. If you would like to informed of Project developments, or order copies of print resources for your ministry, please visit the Kai'Ro Project at: **www.kairoproject.org**

The KaiRo Project is a ministry of Hands of Hur. For more information about Hands of Hur, visit: **www.handsof hur.org**

TABLE OF CONTENTS

PROLOGUE:
DREAMIN'

STORYTELLER: Some folks would say it was a dream. They may be right, but what I witnessed that night truly changed my life. I saw before me a terrible looking prison under a dark night sky. The tall brick walls were topped with twisted coils of razor wire. And from the watchtowers there was a red and hellish glow. I saw an old sign standing out front and in chipped paint it read End of the Road Jail: A Home for the Hopeless: My dream suddenly took me inside and through the shadowy halls until I was taken into a room lined with cells. Inside were men and women, young and old caged like filthy animals. Some of them were chained to walls like leashed dogs. They could hardly move. Others were curled up in the corners of their cells, shivering from the cold and from fear. Many of them were nearly naked. Some were bloody and bruised as if they had been tortured or thrashed by someone. I heard groans and crying. I saw people pressed up against the bars with tears streaming down their faces. There were others bound up like crazy people. They rolled around on the floor or beat their heads against the wall cursing and shouting. Then I saw a young man who looked like he could be no older than eighteen. He was dressed in some baggy jeans, and he was wearing a dirty wife beater. I noticed that he had some bruises on his face and that his knuckles were cracked and bleeding. He was sitting on the ground of his cell and by the small shaft of moonlight coming through his cell window he was writing a letter. It read:

Evangeline,

This may be the last letter I write you for a while, girl. The Preacher stopped in to see me again today and this time I made my decision. Like I said to you this morning when you came by, I think our whole town is about to come to a terrible end. I think all of us are in trouble. The City of Doom is going to be judged. The Preacher broke some things down for me. He told me that if I was willing to get out of town and head out onto the Heavenly Highway that there'd be hope for me for real. I still can't believe you laughed when I told you that. Don't you feel it, girl? Don't you feel that terrible burden on your back? I sure do! It's a burden of guilt, regret, pain, and shame. I started feeling it a long time ago, but I guess I did a good job ignoring it. The Preacher told me that my burden was my soul crying out to be free. He's right. I want to be free for real. And I don't just mean from this lousy jail cell. I want true freedom. The Preacher said the King has the freedom I need and want, and so by the time you find this letter, I'll be gone. My homies Quitter and Follower are getting out of here tomorrow too, and they said they want to go with me. I wish to God that you'd think this thing over and come with me. I'm telling you, Evangeline, this City of Doom that we been living in is going to get burned up. You need to get out while you still can. Come to your senses, girl! I pray you do. If you come looking for me, just follow the dirt road that's past the hedge of bushes at the edge of town. It's a real trail because I've been there once before. Don't waste no more time. You need to come now.

I'll always love you.

Your boy,

Kai'Ro

STORYTELLER: Kai'Ro put the letter in an envelope. He walked over to his cot and picked a black Bible up and started reading it. His lips moved slightly as he read the words. Every now and then he'd stop and stare off; sometimes he'd smile like someone who had just learned some great news. He read and read through the dark of night until the sun started to fill the window of his cell with bright light.

CHAPTER ONE: THE DIRT ROAD

STORYTELLER: In my dream I saw Kai'Ro and two other young men about his age standing on the curb just outside the jail. All three of them were squinting in the noonday sun.

KAI'RO: So, ya'll ready to do this for real?

FOLLOWER: Yeah, man, you know that I'll go wit you wherever you go. I mean, we grew up together in this town, dawg. You think I'm 'bout to just let you roll on outta here by yourself? Naw, I'm goin' wit you.

QUITTER: I mean, I ain't lettin' ya'll just leave me here. I don't understand what all the hype's about, but I'm down.

KAI'RO: Cool. Well, let's go home and clean up, get our things and meet by the hedges on the edge of town.

QUITTER: You mean the ones right off of Excuses Street, right?

KAI'RO: Yeah, those are the ones. Did ya'll write your letters?

STORYTELLER: Quitter and Follower looked at each other and then back at Kai'Ro. Follower cleared his throat.

FOLLOWER: I meant to do it, man, but I fell asleep last night, dawg. My bad. I'll write my girl when we get on the road.

KAI'RO: How 'bout you, Quitter? You write yours?

QUITTER: Naw, homie. I told you my girl would snap on me if I sent her that kinda letter and then went slinkin' out of the house on her. You crazy? I'm just gonna bounce on out of town with ya'll, and that's that. She'll probably just figure I'm off doin' one of my things.

KAI'RO: You should have written your letters. Both of you. I told ya'll, I ain't comin' back here once I'm gone. I love Evangeline as much as you love your girls, but she wasn't down with this whole trip for real. I told her about it every time she came to visit me. She kept laughin' and tellin' me I was just messed up from being locked up. I warned her that I'd do this thing alone. That's why I wrote that letter. She's goin' to have to come after me, 'cause I'm bouncin'.

FOLLOWER: Look, let's just get goin'. I don't want to waste no more time arguin'.

STORYTELLER: The three young men split up and hurried to their homes. When Kai'Ro got to his place he quickly went through the drawers of his dresser. He pulled a small bag out from under his bed and stuffed it with fresh clothes, a small wad of cash that he had hidden, and a black gun from his bottom drawer. After a quick shower, he threw on some baggy jeans, a black tall-T, some shiny Js and a NY cap. He took the letter that he had written in the jail the night before, kissed it, placed it on Evangeline's pillow and then disappeared out the front door. He walked for a while down the sidewalk. The air was hot. A few thuggish looking guys on a porch nodded and waved at him as he passed by. One of them hollered to him.

PAIN: What up, Kai'Ro? So you finally free, dawg?

KAI'RO: Man, I wish.

PAIN: What'cha mean? You out of the joint aren't you?

KAI'RO: No doubt, but my soul ain't free yet. Gotta get my soul freed up.

PAIN: For real? What'cha mean by that? You goin' to go to church or somethin'?

KAI'RO: I can't really explain it yet, dawg. That's why I'm bouncin' up outta here. I'm headin' onto the Heavenly Highway.

PAIN: The Heavenly who…?

KAI'RO: Heavenly Highway, homie. It's gonna lead me to the Cross and it's gonna lead me to the freedom from the burden I got. You know the row of bushes over there where Excuses Street and Bondage Boulevard meet?

PAIN: Yeah. What about it?

KAI'RO: Head through the bushes sometime, playa. You'll find the trail…

STORYTELLER: Kai'Ro smiled at Pain and then waved him good-bye. Pain watched him disappear out of sight. After a few more blocks Kai'Ro came to the wall of bushes that he had described. Quitter and Follower showed up just like they promised.

QUITTER: This is crazy, dawg. I can't believe we're actually doing this.

FOLLOWER: Man, people around here are goin' to flip when they hear what we're doin'.

KAI'RO: The Preacher said we had to move quickly. He said there wasn't much time left. He told me to head out of the City to the Crossroads and then on to the Gate. He said that once I got to the Crossroads I'd have to make a decision to either take the Heavenly Highway or the Path of Least Resistance.

QUITTER: So what's up with the Crossroads? I mean why can't the Preacher dude just tell us which way to go? I don't get it.

KAI'RO: The Preacher said that the Heavenly Highway leads all the way to the City of Gold. But he said every man has to choose for himself.

QUITTER: So is there something wrong with the Path of Least Resistance?

KAI'RO: The Preacher said that the Path of Least Resistance is the easier road to take.

QUITTER: Man, why would we want to make things any harder on ourselves?

KAI'RO: Because the man said that the Path of Least Resistance is wide, flat, and smooth at first, but the further down that road you go you eventually work your way into the Alley of Few Opportunities. He said the Alley is wide at first, but the further you go the tighter it gets. It's gradual, he said, but as you walk down the path the walls of the Alley get closer and closer to the road and after a while the way gets so tight that you actually get stuck and can go nowhere but backwards. He also told me that there are plenty of holes and that a lot of travelers never even make it very far.

FOLLOWER: I'm with Quitter. I don't see how a road with a name like that can be so bad. I bet the Preacher never even went down that road. Some of them Holy Roller guys think it's cool to do things the hard way just so they can feel good about themselves. Know what I'm saying? It's like going uphill is somehow a strategy to get somewhere and to be somebody. Man, I've always found it easier to just chill and to use my brain to find the easiest way to get something done. Why waste my time climbing and clawing when I can be chillin'?

QUITTER: That's for real, dawg.

KAI'RO: I'm just telling you what the Preacher told me. I believe him. I think he was shootin' straight with me.

STORYTELLER: After taking a deep breath Kai'Ro led the way and pushed into the bushes. The other two stopped for a moment and then followed after him. The bushes were thick and thorny and they snagged and pulled at their T-shirts and jeans. Both Quitter and Follower complained as the branches scratched their skin and tore a few holes in their shirts.

QUITTER: Ah c'mon, dawg! This shirt cost me like thirty dollars!

STORYTELLER: Kai'Ro kept going and pushed the branches with his hands until they came out on the other side. As he had promised them a few days earlier there was a small dirt trail that headed off into the countryside. The path was almost invisible and there were a lot of weeds growing on it. Kai'Ro wiped some sweat away from his forehead and waved to his friends to come on. The three walked out into a big, green, open countryside.

KAI'RO: It's nice out here isn't it?

QUITTER: You've been out here before?

KAI'RO: Once. I heard about it so I felt like I had to check it out. I didn't go real far. I had to go back, but, it's nice out. Nice and quiet.

FOLLOWER: Yeah, it smells nice out here too. There's no pollution, graffiti, trash or nothin'.

KAI'RO: The last time I was out here I had only walked a little ways, and then I just sat on that stone over there. I sat there for like an hour, man, and just did nothin'. It's so peaceful. I can't explain it, but I just didn't want to leave. All the plants and the wind in the trees. I guess I never really noticed how nice it is at all until I got out here and actually experienced it. It was just good to get away from all that drama in the city.

QUITTER: Man if it's like this all the way you can count me in, dawg. This is nice out here.

STORYTELLER: The three friends walked for a long time and passed some beautiful places including a deep blue lake, some big rocks, and some woods. They continued to follow the dirt path which was just wide enough for the three of them to walk shoulder to shoulder. At times they walked quietly and sometimes they pointed at all the amazing things around them. After a while they spotted a large building with a tall Vegas-looking sign. The sign read "House of Mockers." Though they were still a ways off, the three men could feel the pound of music and bass hitting them like 18 inch woofers in a '64 Impala on switches. They could also hear the laughter of women. They looked at each other in total surprise trying to figure out what the strange place was all about. They moved closer until the building was right in front of them. It had grey bricks and all of the windows were tinted, but from the outside they could see bright lights flashing behind the glass. In the parking lot outside the House of Mockers were a bunch of young guys and girls laughing, smoking, and carrying on.

FOLLOWER: Yo, what *is* this place? Check out the girls up there.

QUITTER: Man, you ain't playin'. Shoot, homie, I just got the urge to take a 'lil rest. What'cha say, Kai'Ro?

KAI'RO: I think we should keep going. The Preacher said it would take all day to get to the Crossroads, and just beyond the Crossroads was a place for us to rest. I want to get there before dark. The Preacher warned that there are some brothas on this road that we wouldn't want to tangle with after dark. So let's bounce on outta here.

FOLLOWER: Aww, come on Kai'Ro! We could stop in and grab something to drink - maybe get one of these female's digits. How's it going to hurt?

KAI'RO: Listen, Follower, I set out on this journey 'cause the stuff that's going on in that place bothers me. It didn't always used to, but it does now. The Preacher told me I'd have to give that stuff up. The girls, the clubbin', the 40s, all of it. Trust me, I want to go in there too, but when I think about it the burden on my back gets even heavier. I've *got* to get rid of this burden. I've just got to.

STORYTELLER: As Kai'Ro finished speaking, one of the men in the parking lot hollered at them. When he did, all of the others stopped to stare at the three travelers on the path.

PARTYCAT: Yo, is that you Kai'Ro? Man, I ain't see you in the longest.

KAI'RO: Hey, P.C. What's up?

PARTYCAT: Nuttin' much. Man, come up here and have a smoke with us.

KAI'RO: Can't, homie. We're on our way somewhere else.

PARTYCAT: Somewhere else? Where? Man, you've found the only place you need to find right here.

KAI'RO: I don't get down like that no more. Not for real.

PARTYCAT: Man, you're trippin'. I've got three honeys here right now that are just itchin' to dance with you and ya boys. It'll be my treat, my way of saying welcome to the House of Mockers.

FREAKY: Hey, Kai'Ro. Why don't you come up here and come inside. I've never disappointed nobody.

STORYTELLER: Freaky stepped out from behind Partycat. She was wearing some tight shorts, and an even tighter white low-cut T-shirt that exposed her cleavage. She pointed at Kai'Ro and tried to draw him into the House with her finger.

PARTYCAT: You hear the music in there? Man, it's bangin'. Quit wastin' your time out there and get in here and party with me, dawg.

KAI'RO: I appreciate it, man, but we gotta keep goin'. We're off to the Crossroads and then on to the Heavenly Highway.

STORYTELLER: When Kai'Ro told the crew where he and his friends were going the entire parking lot burst into laughter. Some of the girls rolled their eyes. The guys cracked up and pointed at Kai'Ro, Quitter and Follower. Partycat took a long draw from his cigar and blew the smoke out slowly. He glared at Kai'Ro and growled.

PARTYCAT: Now, I know you're trippin'. Since when did Kai'Ro from the City of Doom say no to some dancin' and some sexual healin' with a fine woman?

FREAKY: Yeah, what's your problem, boy? You gay?

KAI'RO: No, I'm not gay. You crazy! I'm just not down with this whole scene no more. I left the City of Doom and I'm off to find life and freedom. So get up off me, I'm fixin' to bounce out of here!

PARTYCAT: Life! Freedom! Man, look around you here, playa! There's no more life and freedom than what you're going to find in this building. Man I've got more life and more freedom waitin' inside then you'll see in a lifetime.

KAI'RO: It's not the same. I want life and freedom for my soul. I've had all that other stuff and it didn't satisfy me. Not for long anyway. I've been to clubs just like this a hundred times. I've had more girls than I can remember. Man, I've done just about anything a dude can do and it left me wantin' more every time. It was like eatin' from a plate every day, but never gettin' enough…always leavin' the table feelin' hungry again. Now I've got an appetite deep inside that's just groaning away. It's a hunger for something that will last forever. I guess you don't understand what kinda freedom I'm talkin' about.

PARTYCAT: Freedom for your soul, huh? A hunger for…man, since when did you get all religious on me? Maybe I oughta come down there and slap some sense into your thick head. Maybe you and your two punk friends ought to step out of here before me and my boys make all of you hurt.

FOLLOWER: Man, bump this! C'mon, Kai'Ro, let's clown this fool. No one's gonna call us no punk! You goin' to let this fool talk to us like this, dawg?

QUITTER: Man, you know I won't back down!

KAI'RO: (holding Follower back) We're on our way, P.C. No need for any hostility. I'm different now. That's why we're leavin'. We're gone.

PARTYCAT: Yeah, get gone, clown. Step on out of here before I change my mind. You and your punk friends won't find anything down that road but loneliness and disappointment.

STORYTELLER: As the three men took off down the trail they were followed by a sea of laughter as the crowd hollered insults at them, cursed them, and mocked them until they were out of sight.

QUITTER: Man, if you weren't one of my best friends I woulda' never gone through all that drama. You didn't do a thing! Man, for real, I was ready to climb up there and knock that cat's head off. He called us punks and faggots and you just stood there! What's happenin' to you?

FOLLOWER: For real, man. I've never seen you like that before. Boys back in the City of Doom would be lookin' for their teeth right now after saying somethin' like that to you. You did nothin' and you made us look like a bunch of girls.

KAI'RO: Look, every inch of me wanted to go in that House with that girl and get inside her pants. And everything that P.C. called us pissed me off, and I was achin' to grab my piece and smoke him right there. No one has called me those names before. *Nobody!* But it's like I said, I don't feel the same. I've got an urge to get to the Crossroad and to get on that Heavenly Highway so that I can lose this wretched burden on my back. It is driving me insane, and it's more important to be free from that burden than anything. Do ya'll not feel one pressin' in on you now?

QUITTER: I feel nothin'. I'm just mad as hell right now.

FOLLOWER: Me too.

STORYTELLER: The House of Mockers experience left the three at odds with one another. The men continued to walk down the path in silence. Kai'Ro led the way as the other two followed behind with their heads hanging. Quitter and Follower no longer seemed too interested in the trip. In time they passed through more open and beautiful spaces, but they paid no attention. Soon they came into a part of the path that disappeared into some tall grass that came up to their shoulders. They got slowed down as Kai'Ro tried hard to keep his eyes on the path. They walked in a line with Follower close at Kai'Ro's heels and Quitter a few steps behind. Suddenly Kai'Ro let out a cry as he and Follower fell into a thick swamp.

FOLLOWER: Man, what in the world? What *is* this?

KAI'RO: I dunno.

FOLLOWER: What do you mean you don't know? Man, I didn't come all this way to fall into no swamp. Heck, naw!

STORYTELLER: Kai'Ro and Follower thrashed around in the water, but the more they thrashed the deeper they sank into the mud.

QUITTER: Man, this is stupid! Look. Grab this stick in my hand and I'll pull ya'll out of there. Let's get back on dry ground and get back home. I can't believe I did this.

FOLLOWER: Yeah. C'mon, Kai'Ro, let's get out of here. This whole trip is a joke, man. I can't believe I let you talk us into this mess.

KAI'RO: I'm not goin' back, ya'll. I can't go back now. The Preacher said we'd go through some stuff. I'm going on to the other side.

STORYTELLER: Follower had turned around and grabbed a hold of the stick that Quitter was holding out to him. Kai'Ro kept thrashing and struggling but he just sunk deeper and deeper. Eventually Follower got out and started scraping the mud and crud off of his clothes with his hands. He began cursing when he looked at his dirty Js and his jeans. Both he and Quitter hollered to Kai'Ro to turn around and join them.

KAI'RO: Look, ya'll don't understand. I'm not going back. I'm going on. I got to go on.

FOLLOWER: Man, now I know what Partycat was sayin' back there. You are a fool. I don't get it, dawg. You're gonna drown out there by yourself. Just turn around and grab a hold of this stick and we'll pull you out.

KAI'RO: Jump in here and join me. It ain't that far to other side. I can see it from here.

STORYTELLER: By now both Follower and Quitter were cursing at their friend and shaking their fists at him. Then they realized his mind wasn't going to change. They waved their hands at him in disgust and took off back towards where they had come. When

Kai'Ro realized that he was all alone he tried even harder to get to the other side, but he just kept sinking deeper and deeper. I could see that he was starting to panic. The mud in the swamp was sucking him down. He called out for help and held up his arms. Just then a man came running towards him.

HELPER: Hold on! Don't give up!

STORYTELLER: A man came running on a stone path just beside the marsh. He got right up on Kai'Ro and then extended him a hand to pull him out. With a big tug he hauled Kai'Ro out of the mud. Kai'Ro fell down on the ground and started gasping.

HELPER: You'll be alright, brotha! Why didn't you take the stone path?

KAI'RO: (coughing) Man, I didn't see it for real. I was just walking along, and then all of a sudden I fell in that awful swamp.

HELPER: The Swamp of Discouragement has gotten a lot of brothas early in their trip to the Heavenly Highway. A lot of dudes get stuck, give up, and never come back. Did you come alone?

KAI'RO: No. I had two of my best friends with me, but they went back and left me alone.

HELPER: A lot of people lose heart at this terrible swamp. The King has built this stone path alongside it for travelers like you, but the mud often shifts, the grass grows high, and the path is hard to find.

KAI'RO: I couldn't see it for nuthin'.

HELPER: Don't get discouraged, dawg. Your eyes are new to this path, As you keep goin' on this journey your eyes will grow and you will get used to seein' the blessings and little helpful things the King has left for you.

STORYTELLER: Kai'Ro stood up and started swiping the mud and slime off of his pants and shirt.

KAI'RO: I just feel stupid. I feel real stupid.

HELPER: The fact that you kept going shows courage, and it shows that you're committed. I'm glad I was here. The King has kept me here to help out brothas like you when they get stuck.

KAI'RO: Thanks.

HELPER: No problem. Now get goin'. There's still time left in the day.

STORYTELLER: Kai'Ro shook Helper's hand and then headed off again alone. He walked for a while down the dirt path. I could tell that he was thinking hard.

CHAPTER TWO:
WORLDLY WISEMAN

STORYTELLER: After a while I could see a man coming towards Kai'Ro from the opposite direction. The man was dressed in a flashy green and black suit. He had alligator boots, shiny rimmed glasses, and a cane. He was wearing a big gold chain with a cross on it. He came towards Kai'Ro and started talking to him.

WORLDLY WISEMAN: Yo, what's good, son? The name's Worldly Wiseman.

KAI'RO: W'sup?

WW: What happened to you? You look like you got it rough, man.

KAI'RO: Yeah, I fell into the Swamp of Discouragement back there. It's all good now.

WW: The Swamp of Discouragement? Man, where you headin' playa?

KAI'RO: I'm heading to the Crossroads and then on to the Gate to the Heavenly Highway.

WW: (laughing) So my man got some religion, huh? Who put the Heavenly Highway in your head, son?

KAI'RO: The Preacher.

WW: Man, that old fool? Son, that man ain't worth the cheap suits he wears to church on Sunday. He's got you confused. Let me ask you something. You got a girl?

KAI'RO: Yeah. I got a girl back home

WW: You just left her back there, man? Why? She did you wrong or something?

KAI'RO: No, it wasn't like that. She was a good girl. I mean she and I were real tight.

WW: Were you good to her, or did you have a little play goin' on on the side, man?

KAI'RO: Naw, it wasn't like that. We were both real true to each other. I just had to move on. I've got this doggone burden on my back, and until I get free of it, there just ain't no peace for me for real.

WW: I 'spose the Preacher told you about the burden too.

KAI'RO: Yeah, but…

WW: You left your girl and all your friends because you was listenin' to the Preacher? Boy, you must be crazy.

KAI'RO: Yeah? A lot of people have been tellin' me that, but what's drivin' me crazy is this burden. I mean, this burden keeps me up nights. Besides, he wasn't the only one who got me going on this road. He was just the final spark.

WW: What you mean?

STORYTELLER: Kai'Ro reached into his pants pocket and pulled out an old and tattered black book.

KAI'RO: I been reading this Bible. This was my granddad's. He gave it to my Pops, but my Pops didn't read it much. He split when I was three and the book stayed in my Mama's bedroom for years. She used to read it to us every now and then, but not much. I started readin' in it a few months ago, and it's been saying the same thing as The Preacher. It says I got a real problem inside. It says in there that I offend God with my sin. It even says that my town and everything that I know is going to get burned up and me along with it unless I get rid of this burden.

WW: (Laughing) Man, that ol' Preacher and that book has got you scared, bro. There's a lot of brothas and sistas that come down this way complaining about their burden, and they go on yappin' about how they're going to the Crossroads and on to the Heavenly Highway. Man, I got a way to get rid of that burden and you don't have to go to all that trouble and go on and waste all your time.

KAI'RO: Whatcha' mean, man?

WW: Do you see that hill over there?

STORYTELLER: Kai'Ro turned to his left and saw a tall grassy hill. On the top there were several large houses. He stared at the hill for a while.

KAI'RO: What about that hill?

WW: I got a friend up there, man. He specializes in removing those burdens.

KAI'RO: What are you talking about?

WW: His name is Mac-Morality, and that little suburb up there, man, that's Legalopolis. My boy Mac specializes in removing burdens. He's been doing it for a real long time. Most of those folks up there were travelers just like you. All of them were complaining about this "burden" and how they just had to get rid of it. They were on their way to the Heavenly Highway when they met Mac and got things straightened out by him.

STORYTELLER: It was clear to me that Kai'Ro's mind was spinning. He stared at Worldly Wiseman like he didn't know if he could trust him. I wondered what decision he would make.

KAI'RO: That sounds good, but what you're saying doesn't sound at all like what The Preacher said.

WW: Look, you need to forget The Preacher. He's a looney old man that's filled a lot of people's heads with nothin' but trouble and guilt. Mac is all about giving people peace and giving it to them fast. Listen, what you're missing is balance. You almost had it back in the City of Doom, but you were a little off, man. Sounds to me like you had it goin' on. You have a good girl. She's good to you and you're good to her. That's all that matters for real. Keep your nose clean. Stay out of the real deep stuff, you know, the type of stuff that will get you in trouble. You're almost there already, man. Mac will set you straight. Shoot, maybe you and your girl can leave that city of yours and all that drama behind. You'll get a new perspective up there on Legalopolis. Ya'll could move up there.

KAI'RO: Well, I want to get rid of this burden. It's killing me. I'll head up there and talk to ya boy, Mac. If he can set me straight, then I'm game.

STORYTELLER: Worldly Wiseman flashed a big gold toothed smile and slapped Kai'Ro on the back.

WW: That's what I'm talking about! When Mac sets you straight you'll be looking me up to say 'thank you.'

KAI'RO: I appreciate it. I'll holler at you.

STORYTELLER: With that, Kai'Ro turned off the dirt trail and headed for the green hill. But when he got there it was much steeper and scarier than it first seemed. In fact when he came to the bottom, it almost seemed to bend up and over him. As he looked at the hill he noticed a small trail that zigzagged back and forth along the front of it. He put his foot forward but it was slick so he leaned forward to brace himself with his hand. He cried out as one of the stones cut his hand. He tried again, but his burden and the awkwardness of the path itself made the going real hard. He was only able to get a few feet up the path and then he tripped and he stumbled and fell down to the bottom. He got real mad and punched the ground. As he looked up he saw The Preacher coming towards him. Embarrassed, he hung his head.

PREACHER: Son, what are you doing here?

KAI'RO: I was told that I could lose my burden up there. I thought it sounded like a good idea.

PREACHER: And who told you *that?*

KAI'RO: Worldly Wiseman told me there was a man up there named Mac-Morality who could free me of this burden by helping me balance and order my life. It sounded good. It even sounded…

PREACHER: Did it really sound good to you, son? I mean deep down in your soul, did it sound good?

KAI'RO: (Sighing) Not for real. I mean, yeah, it sounded good to my ears to get free of this burden, but in my soul, it didn't sit right.

PREACHER: Things are changing in you, Kai'Ro. You aren't seeing and hearing things the same any more, are you? Your soul wants freedom and that freedom isn't going to come on the top of that hill. Didn't Helper promise you that as you journeyed down the road that you'd begin to see things differently?

KAI'RO: Yeah.

PREACHER: You will have to be careful because there are others more cunning than Worldly Wiseman who will seek to take you off the path. Some will make pleasant promises that will be nothing but lies. Others will seek to destroy you entirely, my son. Let me show you something.

STORYTELLER: The Preacher walked a little ways along the edge of the hill to some tall grass. Kai'Ro followed close by. The Preacher parted some of the grass and showed Kai'Ro a large pile of bricks, a shattered window frame, a busted door, and what looked like a bed mattress, some cabinets, and a kitchen table. It was the ruins of an old house.

PREACHER: Do you know where all this stuff came from?

STORYTELLER: Kai'Ro looked at The Preacher for a minute and then took a hard look up towards the top of the hill.

PREACHER: Yes, son. That house was once up there. The top of that hill is nothing but brittle rock and sand. Those who do make it up there find the view to be splendid, but when the winds start to blow or a violent storm whips across the hill, many of those houses come tumbling down. There are many more fallen houses just like this one scattered all around this hill. Mac and his ilk are selling nothing but lies. They can't free you or anyone from their burden, and the life they offer is a myth.

KAI'RO: I was wrong to doubt you. I'm sorry.

PREACHER: You were wrong to doubt the truth. Knowing the truth is what's going to set you free.

KAI'RO: I'm only a day into this thing, and I got harassed by a bunch of guys and girls back down the way. My two homeboys left me high and dry. Then I fell and almost sank in a swamp of Discouragement. I'm tired already. This walk is a beast for real.

PREACHER: It is a beast. Yet, when you get to the foot of the Cross and your burden rolls away you will know and taste life as never before. I can't put it any plainer than that. The tug in your heart is real. It's a tug for life. *Abundant* life. Listen, only the Cross can free your burden for real. Nothing else will work. Nothing.

KAI'RO: Well, I best be going then. Maybe I can make it to the Crossroads before it gets dark.

PREACHER: You're almost there already. Goodwill at the Gate will take you in for the night. Peace be unto you my son.

STORYTELLER: Kai'Ro said his goodbyes and then hurried along on the dirt trail again. He moved quickly because he knew that he had to make up his lost time. He walked along for quite a while. Sometimes he'd hum, and other times he'd throw on his headphones and bob his head to one of the tracks he had made in the studio. After some time he came over a small hill and then to a sudden fork in the road. An old beat-up sign pointed to a wide and well-traveled road to the left. The words on the sign read THE PATH OF LEAST RESISTANCE. This road was smooth, paved, and level as far as the eye could see. To the right was a narrow road just wide enough for a man and a friend. The sign for this road read HEAVENLY HIGHWAY. This path was bumpy, full of twists and turns, and it was so steep that Kai'Ro groaned. It looked similar to the path on the hill leading up to Legalopolis, but it appeared to me much less traveled. Kai'Ro paused for just a moment to catch his breath. He looked for a few moments at THE PATH OF LEAST RESISTANCE but then shook his head. With quick strides he headed up THE HEAVENLY HIGHWAY.

CHAPTER THREE:
THE GATE &
GOODWILL

STORYTELLER: I could tell that Kai'Ro was ready to get to the Gate. He half-jogged down the dirt road until it suddenly turned into cracked blacktop. The sun was fading in the sky overhead and the light along the road was growing dimmer. Suddenly he came up on a long wall that blocked him from going further. A big thick wooden gate stood directly in front of him. He pulled on it but the door wouldn't budge. He rapped a large iron knocker and beat the door with the flat of his hand.

GOODWILL: Who goes there?

KAI'RO: It's me, Kai'Ro, from the City of Doom.

GOODWILL: Why do you come to the Gate?

KAI'RO: Man, I'm here to get on that Heavenly Highway and to get rid of this terrible burden.

GOODWILL: Then we don't have a lot of time, do we?

STORYTELLER: With that the Gate was thrown open and a strong arm grabbed Kai'Ro and yanked him through the opening.

KAI'RO: Yo, take it easy! What'cha grabbin' me for, dawg?

GOODWILL: Sorry, brother, but just beyond this wall is one of Diablo's Towers. He has expert marksmen up there who'd love to snipe a brother dead just before he comes through the gate. The whole door of this Gate is tore up with bullet holes. I'm surprised you didn't see the holes.

KAI'RO: (straightening his shirt) Naw, it's gettin' dark. I didn't see the holes, but thanks for pullin' me in. You just surprised me, that's all.

GOODWILL: No big deal. So, you headin' for the Mountain of the Cross?

KAI'RO: Yeah.

GOODWILL: (laughing joyously) This is wonderful news! Aw, man, you gotta stay with me tonight. We gotta talk.

KAI'RO: I really should keep goin'. I lost some time today talkin' to the wrong brotha.

GOODWILL: Man, you don't want to get on this Highway in the dark. There's some crazy cats out at night. You can get up early.

KAI'RO: Appreciate it.

STORYTELLER: I could see that Goodwill had a little house just beyond the Gate. Inside he had a small living room with a couch and two chairs. There was a kitchen, and a bathroom and bedroom. You could see all of these things from the front door. Goodwill told Kai'Ro to have a seat. He offered him a sandwich out of the fridge and the two began to talk.

KAI'RO: (in between bites) So, what'cha doing at this Gate?

GOODWILL: I feel in my spirit that I just gotta help draw people in. You'd be surprised how many people make it all the way to the Gate. Sometimes I can hear them shufflin' their feet on the other side and then just change their minds. Some of 'em reach for the handle and get hit by one of the snipers bullets. Some get shot dead, and others get hurt so badly they limp home angry and messed up. The Spirit Himself tugs a lot of sistas and brothas like yourself to the Gate, but it takes a step of faith and courage to really go for it. Know what I mean? I gotta give some cats that extra tug or push or whatever it takes.

KAI'RO: Like you did with me…

GOODWILL: Exactly. So, you know what you're gettin' in for on this journey?

KAI'RO: Man, I just want to get rid of this burden. If I can do that then I'll be straight.

GOODWILL: Yeah, you'll be 'straighter,' but it ain't over.

KAI'RO: (putting down his sandwich) What'cha mean it ain't over?

GOODWILL: I mean, it's over for that burden on your back, but the journey ain't over. You gotta walk this road all the way to the City of Gold. It don't stop until you get there…

KAI'RO: The Preacher told me all that. That's where I'm headin'… to the City of Gold in case you're wonderin'. My main thing is to get rid of this burden because it's drivin' me mad for real.

GOODWILL: Well, you're almost there, dawg. Tell me how you found out 'bout that burden.

KAI'RO: I used to be up in church every Sunday since I was a boy. My grandmom and moms used to drag me up there every week. I sang in the choir, ushered, and all that. I was a pretty good kid, but you know, when I got older I got mixed up in some thangs. I started rollin' with some boys that was real hard. I mean we got into some stuff. We stole stuff from stores. Smoked a little. I started stealin' from my moms. Started hustlin'. Got in a lot of fights, homie. Yeah…a whole lot a fights. Started carryin' a piece. I used it a coupl'a times, but don't know if I ever killed nobody. Man, it kinda all became like one of those blurry dreams you know? I just remember not feelin' nothin' at all. I'd go to bed at night numb and just stare at the ceiling. I saw two of my boys get shot. One of 'em died and I didn't even cry at his funeral. I was kinda dead myself I think. My moms used to try to talk to me and I just wouldn't say nothin' at all.

GOODWILL: Sounds like God was backin' you up against a wall for real.

KAI'RO: Yeah, it was something like that. I moved out of the house when I was seventeen and moved in with my girl, Evangeline. She was good to me. We were doin' alright. One night me and two of my boys got arrested for fightin' at a club. I beat up three guys real bad. I got pretty messed up myself. I was sittin' in a jail cell mad and hurtin' all over. That's when I met the Preacher. He showed up out of nowhere and just talked to me through the bars for like two hours or something. I tuned him out at first 'cause I didn't like those holy roller preachers, but there was something about this guy. His eyes were full of fire, you know. He had that fire that fighters have, but at the same time they were full of some kind of peace. He just stared at me and I felt like he was seein' deep into my heart for real. He told me that I was on a path to death and that God in His mercy and love had spared me again and again. I don't know how he knew, but he listed like three or four things that happened to me, and I had never met him before. He told me that God's goodness and kindness should lead me to repentance, but that instead I was hardenin' my heart. He was right, dawg. There were like three or four times where I should have died for real. I got in a nasty car wreck one time when I was real drunk. My car got crushed up on a telephone pole like a Coke can and I just walked away with hardly a scratch. I was at a party one night when some dudes got in a fight and started firin' off shots inside the house. Everybody started runnin.' The cat next to me got dropped. He got paralyzed…it was like God was lookin' out for me the whole time and I just wasn't payin' him no attention. Lookin' back…me survivin' those things was no coincidence.

GOODWILL: You're right. God was screamin' for your attention and tryin' to show you how much He loved you.

KAI'RO: Yeah. The Preacher told me that my lifestyle offended God, but he also said that the King loved me and died for me. He told me that my life deserved Hell, but that the King took Hell for me on the Cross. This cut me deep. I was like 'whoa.' I was just listen' so hard and I didn't want him to stop talkin' about this stuff. I had heard religion before, but this guy was breakin' stuff down on a whole different level for me. He told me that my City was headed for destruction and that I'd go down with it if I didn't get on this Heavenly Highway.

GOODWILL: So when'd you notice the burden?

KAI'RO: I don't remember exactly. I mean, I think it had always kinda been there in the back of my mind…botherin' me. Somewhere around the time he told me that I deserved Hell and that I offended God I started feeling weighed down and desperate. I felt like I had to bust out of that jail. I just felt trapped and terrified too.

While I was in there, I talked to my girl about what the Preacher said, but she laughed at me every time I brought it up. I asked her if she wanted to go to the Heavenly Highway with me and get rid of her burden too. She always just looked at me crazy and she'd say, 'What burden, boy?' I knew then that I'd have to do something for real even if it meant going by myself. I had to say goodbye to that thug life. So, here I am…

GOODWILL: That's deep, homie. Thanks for sharin' that with me. It's funny 'cause almost everybody's got a different story for why they come to the Gate, but everybody's got one thing in common… that doggone burden.

KAI'RO: Can't wait to lose it forever. I know I'll feel so good.

GOODWILL: There are still some struggles you'll be facin' on your way to the Mountain of the Cross. You've got to be careful. Real careful.

KAI'RO: What'cha mean?

GOODWILL: The Heavenly Highway has all kinds of cats on it. Some of them are heading to the City of Gold like you, but there's a lot that are there just frontin', and they're some dangerous dudes. They'll pull you off the path real quick if you aren't careful.

KAI'RO: What'cha mean frontin'?

GOODWILL: They're imposters, man. They're like wolves in sheep's clothing. They talk a good game you know? But they don't walk it at all. Some of them are just 'religious.' They talk church talk and they even wear the church clothes, but they stink like the world because that's how they're livin'.

KAI'RO: That used to be me. I mean that's how I lived until I started feelin' this burden.

GOODWILL: They're a more dangerous animal. Most of these guys know about the burden but they moved past it. It's like they've discovered how to block it out and just move on. They've got hard hearts. When you find out about the burden, and then move past it it's like you've reached a whole new level of evil. The Spirit sticks our heart and we recognize our bad lives, and then we can go one of two directions. In your case, man, you said enough is enough. You're headin' to the Cross. A lot of guys just say, 'That's alright. I can live with this thing. I can do my thing.' It's tragic, man. It's like they've got a deep hunger for Hell. They want Hell. They're goin' get Hell.

KAI'RO: I hear you. I know some guys like that. I don't understand it, dawg. I'm one of those guys who can't live with the fact that somethin's broken. I just got to fix it. When I heard there was a cure to my burden and my sin problem I just had to go out and find it.

GOODWILL: (standing up) Be sure to stop by the Interpreter's place when you get there. You'll run into his place on your way, and he'll be sure to explain some things to you that will help you on your way.

KAI'RO: That sounds good. I'll be sure to look him up.

GOODWILL: Yeah, well, you need to rest. You've got a big day ahead of you tomorrow.

KAI'RO: Sounds good.

CHAPTER FOUR: CHURCHBOY

STORYTELLER: When Kai'Ro woke up the next morning he looked better. He and Goodwill had some bacon, eggs and grits for breakfast. They talked for a little bit, but Kai'Ro wanted to get going so he told Goodwill thanks and then took off onto the road again. The morning air was cool and Kai'Ro was moving quickly. He moved down the road for a while until he spotted a small white church off to the side. The church was called Church of the Sunday Morning Faithful. The sign said the church was run by Pastor Dualist. Kai'Ro squinted his eyes for a minute at the sign but kept going. After a while he saw a lanky man leaning against a tree smoking a Black 'n Mild. The guy had a large red tall-t, a backwards ball cap and large gold chain around his neck with a diamond studded skull. Kai'Ro nodded at the man hoping he could just pass him by.

CHURCHBOY: What's up, playa?

KAI'RO: What's up…

CHURCHBOY: Hold on, man. Where you goin'?

KAI'RO: I'm headin' to the Mountain of the Cross down the road a ways from here.

CHURCHBOY: (Takes a long drag from his cigar) Yeah? That's cool. I'm a religious guy too.

STORYTELLER: I could tell that Kai'Ro wanted to keep going, but he stopped to give the man a moment of his time.

CHURCHBOY: You probably passed my church back there.

KAI'RO: You go to that "Church of the Sunday Morning Faithful?"

CHURCHBOY: Yeah, homie. I'm one of the deacons there.

KAI'RO: For real?

CHURCHBOY: Yeah. I've been goin' there my whole life. My girl sings in the choir.

KAI'RO: You married?

CHURCHBOY: (laughing) Naw, dawg. It ain't like that. Can't tie this boy down for real. I mean we been livin' together for 'bout three years, but I can't see myself gettin' married for real.

KAI'RO: And you're a deacon at your church?

CHURCHBOY: Shoot! I preach sometimes. I sing sometimes. I usher. I do it all. I'm up there every Sunday doin' my thing for the church.

KAI'RO: So, what do you do for a job?

CHURCHBOY: (flicking some ash on the ground) I got a little club I run down the way. It's called Saturday Fire. It's slammin' every Friday and Saturday, dawg. You should see the shorties dancin' up in there. It's off the chain!

KAI'RO: Naw, I don't do that scene no more.

CHURCHBOY: What'cha talkin about, playa? Every dude loves a good club where he can meet some ladies and get a little somethin' to drink. What'cha mean you don't do that scene no more?

KAI'RO: That whole scene is played out, dawg. I mean I used to be up in the club all the time. I just can't do that no more. That stuff just makes me depressed now. I mean it's off the chain while I'm there, but when I get home I just feel empty inside.

CHURCHBOY: (chuckling) Man, that's messed up. How does a guy come home feelin' empty after chillin' with his boys and dancin' with some fine women? That's crazy, dude!

KAI'RO: Yeah, maybe. I'm tryin' to figure how a dude can go from clubbin' on Saturday night to preachin' a sermon the next morning at his church. That's what I'm tryin' to figure out.

CHURCHBOY: (waving his hand at Kai'Ro) That ain't no big deal. Like I said, I'm religious, man. I do my thing for the church.

There ain't nothin' wrong with doing what I do. You judgin' me or somethin'?

KAI'RO: No, it's not like that. I'm not judgin' you. But from what I've been readin', God will judge you for being two-faced. The Word calls what you're doin' bein' a 'hypocrite,' and every time that word appears…some bad stuff follows. I'm just tellin' you that I don't think you can keep both of those lives up forever. I mean, I did it for a while, but when I started readin' this book and started listenin' with my heart I could see that I had a real problem. I started feelin' a real burden on my back, and once I heard how I could get rid of it, I took off on this road I'm on. You ever heard of the Mountain of the Cross?

CHURCHBOY: I mean, I've heard of it. I've never been there for real, but I believe in it and everything. Pastor Dualist always tells us just to make it to church, keep our tithe comin', and stay away from the really bad stuff. I put something in the plate each Sunday. You feel me?

KAI'RO: That's how I was too for a long time, but a Preacher told me that I couldn't keep livin' like I was. He said that my life was lost in darkness, and it was, dawg. He said that I could walk in the light, but he told me I couldn't have it both ways. I couldn't keep doin' my thing in the dark and then try to get back in the light each Sunday. He said I'd need to get to the Cross where my sins could be forgiven and I could experience life for real for the first time. He said there I'd find the power in the King to change. That's what I want, and that's where I'm goin'.

CHURCHBOY: I don't like that word 'sin.' I mean, who's to really say what it is for real? I just try to be a good person and get to church. I've never killed anyone, and it ain't like I deal dope or nothin' like that…I mean we all sin don't we? You're no different than me. You sin too.

KAI'RO: I know I do, but I'm sick of it, homie. You don't seem to be sick of it and it don't seem to bother you. I feel guilt in my soul when I do those old things…why don't you feel no guilt? I just can't live it up six days a week and then try to get religious one day a week. I want to have the power to change. I believe I'm going to find it at the Cross. You should come with me, homie.

CHURCHBOY: Like I said, dude, I don't see the big difference. I go to church and do my best. Ain't nobody perfect. I don't see how I gotta give up certain things in my life and make my life harder and all that…some of them real religious cats have no fun at all, dawg. It's like they can't do nothin' fun.

KAI'RO: I guess that's where we're different then. I mean, from what I understand my life is going to get easier 'cause I'm going to get rid of this burden and live a life of freedom. I want freedom, dawg. I'm talkin' 'bout real freedom…not just the freedom to do what I want because that whole life runs dry. I'm talkin' about the freedom from being empty and depressed and angry all the time… freedom to live life the way it's 'sposed to be lived…I mean, imagine if everybody could obey just one of the 10 Commandments. Like what if everybody stopped killin'? I mean everybody, dawg. Don't you think that would make the world a better place? Don't you think if everybody obeyed that one commandment it would help us all live a little more the way we're 'sposed to live? I think God has given us rules not 'cause He wants to take away our joy but because He wants to protect us from losin' that joy through our own foolishness 'n mistakes. He wants us to find our joy in Him and in followin' Him down the road He walked when He was on earth.

CHURCHBOY: Yeah. I guess we're just different. I feel like I'm livin' and I'm happy with my life. To each his own, playa. To each his own.

KAI'RO: I used to say that too. We'll see, dawg. I gotta keep movin' on to the Mountain of the Cross. Peace.

CHURCHBOY: We'll see you around. Feel free to swing by my church on Sunday. I think you'll be feelin' it.

KAI'RO: Don't think so, homie. I hope you think about what I said. Peace.

CHAPTER FIVE:
THE INTERPRETER'S HOUSE

STORYTELLER: Kai'Ro waved goodbye to Churchboy and continued down the road. He went on for a little while until he came to a mailbox that said: "The Interpreter." He stopped and stared down the long driveway. There was a big house with large windows. Kai'Ro remembered Goodwill's words and he took off down the driveway until he came up on the Interpreter's door. After he knocked an older man answered the door. He had a very wrinkled face and dark brown eyes. He smiled.

INTERPRETER: Can I help you, pilgrim?

KAI'RO: Yeah, my name is Kai'Ro and I was told by Goodwill to stop by and see you. He said that you would show me some things and explain them to me.

INTERPRETER: If you are a traveler in search of wisdom then you have come to the right place and I'll be happy to show you some things. Please come in.

STORYTELLER: The Interpreter took Kai'Ro into the house. I was surprised to see how big it was. There were many many rooms and each one had a closed door. The Interpreter waved his hand at Kai'Ro to come on, and they moved together towards a big red door.

INTERPRETER: (opening the door) Come and and let me show you this. I'd like for you to see Patience and Passion.

STORYTELLER: When they went into a room I saw two boys sitting at different tables. They must have been about eight or nine years old. One of the boys sat quietly at his table looking at a beautiful picture. It was a picture of the ocean with blue-green waters, shining white sand, and all kinds of big green palm trees. It was an amazing picture. The kid just looked at it with a big smile and sometimes he'd touch the picture with his hands like he was trying to imagine how cool a place like that must really be.

I looked at the other boy. He had his head in his hands and he kept rolling his eyes and sighing real loud. He had the same picture as the first boy but after looking at it for just a few seconds he pushed it off the table and onto the floor. Every now and then he'd look up at a clock on the wall and then sigh again. Just then a fat and dirty looking man came in carrying a big grey bucket of sand. He walked up to the boy and poured it out on the table. The boy smiled and started playing with the sand. He was having fun and started building a castle with it. But every time he got a few parts of it built, it would just fall apart and he'd have to start all over. He was getting frustrated. This happened a whole bunch of times and he got more and more angry, but he kept on trying even though it wouldn't work. Then, all of a sudden a huge gust of wind blew all of his sand off of the table. As it did, a nicely dressed woman with a face like an angel came into the room and walked up to the other boy and spoke to him. "Are you ready to go, child?" she asked him. "Are we going here?" the boy asked excitedly as he pointed at his picture. "Yes we are," she said with a smile. Then she took the happy child by the hand and they left together. I saw the other boy with his sand scattered all over the floor and he was crying his eyes out.

INTERPRETER: What do you see here, son?

KAI'RO: I'm not sure I understand. I mean, I'm pretty sure that the kid with the painting is Patience because it was like he was just waiting and waiting patiently to get up and go to that beautiful beach. That other boy was just all restless and whinin'. I'm pretty sure he's Passion.

INTERPRETER: You're right about that, but let's look at these two boys a few years down the road. I think you'll understand better then.

STORYTELLER: There was a large green door at the back of the room and the two stepped through it. I saw a young man in his early thirties sitting at a large wooden table. Across from him was a beautiful woman. The two of them were smiling at one another. I noticed gold wedding rings on both of their hands. At the table with them were three children. The children were laughing and carrying on in a joyful way. Then the man at the table asked them all to be quiet and they all bowed their heads and prayed. It was a pretty long prayer with many thank yous to God for all His blessings and provisions. When he was finished they passed around several dishes full of delicious looking meats and greens. There was so much happiness at the table as all five of them talked with one another. Every now and then the man would look up at his wife and just smile or wink at her. There was a lot of love at that table.

INTERPRETER: Come, Kai'Ro, and let's look at something else.

STORYTELLER: The two of them left and walked through an old beat up door into a dank and musty room that smelled like old cigarettes and sweat. I saw a young man in the middle of the room standing there with a big smile on his face. He had on some real baggy jeans, a black baseball cap, and a black tall-t with a skull and crossbones on the front of it. Just then a real scandalous looking girl in a tight bright red dress walked into the room. They talked for a minute and then started kissing. Then she disappeared. From the other side of the room another girl walked into the room in a short black skirt. She smiled at him in a real seductive kind of way and just like with the first girl they started making out real passionately. She disappeared too. Another girl came in and then another, and then another, and this went on until I lost count. There was a bright flash and I saw the man in the corner of the room smoking a joint with a couple of homies. There was another flash and I saw him in a different part of the room drinking something out of a crumpled paper sack. Then there were two more flashes with more girls and kissing and then there was one big flash and I saw the man in the middle of the room with a crazy look on his face. All of a sudden six children of different ages came into the room. Three of the littlest ones either crawled or walked up to him and were pulling on his pants legs trying to get him to hold them or play with him. Two slightly older ones just kind of stared at him wondering if he was going to look at them or even talk to them. The oldest one, a girl, just glared at him with her arms folded across her chest. There was a flash and then they were gone. The doors in the room opened and most of the different girls that I had seen earlier came into the room hollering and fussing at him. Some of them were screaming at him, asking him for their money. Others cursed at him and told him he was a no good daddy. A few of them slapped him and hit him in an awful way. There was a final flash and I saw the man hunched up in the corner of the room with his knees pulled up to his chest. His clothes were all raggedy and he looked skinny and weak. I could tell that he was real sick. He just dropped his head onto his knees and started crying like a baby.

INTERPRETER: Maybe now you understand, son?

KAI'RO: I think so, but why don't you explain it to me a little bit.

INTERPRETER: Passion couldn't wait for the promises and delights of God's heavenly Kingdom. He wanted all of his delight now. Both of those little boys in the first room were promised a trip to that amazing beach and Patience was willing to wait for that promise. In fact he put so much hope and trust in that promise that he found joy even in the waiting. Passion wanted his pleasure now so the closest thing he could get was a bucket full of dried up sand. There's nothing you can do with a bucket of sand. He thought it was cool for a while, but once he realized he could do nothing with it he got mad and frustrated. It's sad, but a lot of people trade heaven and the promises of God's joy for a bucket of lousy sand. In God's presence there is fulness of joy and at His right hand pleasures forever more. This is an enormous promise for this life and the next. But many reject this promise and choose to live outside of the King's presence. Yet those who are cast from His presence will experience an empty and painful life, as well as eternal punishment in Hell.

KAI'RO: It seems crazy that someone would trade a trip to a place as tight as that one in the picture for a bucket of dried-up sand.

INTERPRETER: Well, it is a form of craziness. It's called a depraved mind and a lot of people have one. When someone decides to turn their back on God and starts shaking their fist at His Word, He hands them over to their own ways and desires. But see, there's a way that seems right to a man but in the end it leads to death. When any man is handed over to his own desires and lusts he finds himself in a terrible place like Passion did.

Think about the other room. You saw Patience eating a joyful dinner with his family. You see, Patience waited for the right woman. He got teased a lot growing up, but he trusted in God's commandments to wait until he got married to have sex. He was tempted like anyone else, but he hung on. He found the girl of his dreams in college, got married, landed a great job, and as you saw God provided him and his wife with three beautiful children. Patience waited and obeyed what God told him to do.

KAI'RO: Yeah, his beautiful family was sorta like a beautiful beach…

INTERPRETER: Now you're starting to get it. Passion had heard God's commands and heard about the promises but he wanted all of his pleasure immediately. He found a lot of fine women and had a lot of fun times for a while. But as time went on his life started to fall apart. He got a bunch of girls pregnant, got involved in the fleeting pleasures of drugs, drinking, and partying. It was a good time for him for a short while, but one day he woke up with six kids looking at him to be a daddy he wasn't willing or ready to be. All those girls came to him looking for child support and the poor man was broke. The drugs and drinking took a toll on his health and so did all that sex. The poor guy just wasted away. He missed out on all the promises that Patience waited for to come true.

KAI'RO: (shaking his head) Man, did he ever miss out. That coulda' been me. I was livin' like him for a while. But not no more.

INTERPRETER: Come on. There's more to see.

STORYTELLER: The two men walked into the hallway and the Interpreter led Kai'Ro through a thick brown wooden door. There they watched a young woman out in an open field. She was on her hands and knees digging in the ground when she came upon a great fortune. It was one of the most beautiful and shiny treasures I had ever seen. The woman's face was filled with joy as she looked at it. As fast as she could, she got up and raced to her house. I watched as she furiously gathered all her things together. She snatched a small box of jewelry, all of her CDs, an iPod, her computer, a whole bunch of clothes and other items. Everything she owned she tossed into boxes. She carried everything down to her car and drove to a large market where she sold everything. Finally, she even traded in her car and got rid of her apartment. She walked away from everything she owned. With her money clutched tightly in her hand, she walked to a real estate place called Kingdom Property. She handed a man there all the money she held in her hand. Then the man gave her a deed to some property. A huge smile brightened her face and she took off running again back to where the treasure was found. With joy and excitement she pulled the valuable fortune out of the ground. It was a million times more priceless than any of the things she had sold and given up.

INTERPRETER: This one is not so hard to understand. The treasures of the Kingdom are like the treasure in that field. In that field she found true peace, hope, life and joy. When this young woman found this treasure, she gave up everything she had to have it. She understood its full value and that the treasures, the cars, clothing, jewelry and possessions of this world paled in comparison. How many people have it the other way around?

KAI'RO: Most everybody does.

INTERPRETER: This woman put the treasures of the Kingdom first. And, we *all* have to do that if we want to receive it. If we store up our treasures here on earth, then we don't really want the Kingdom. We just want to pretend that we do. Don't be fooled. The treasures of this earth are powerful things that can pull you away, son.

KAI'RO: I feel you.

INTERPRETER: (smiling and putting his hand on Kai'Ro's shoulder) Let's look at another thing. Follow me.

STORYTELLER: They walked a ways down the hall and passed many rooms. Kai'Ro stopped to stare at one of the paintings that was hanging on the wall.

KAI'RO: What's *this* painting all about?

INTERPRETER: (smiling) That is a painting that has stopped many travelers. We'll come back and look at it before you leave.

KAI'RO: Cool.

STORYTELLER: The Interpreter walked to another door and they went through it. The first thing I saw was an amazing white castle that had towers rising high up into the sky. Big flags with crosses on them were snapping in the wind. The castle had light bursting from it like sun fire. As I looked down I saw a gang of angry looking thugs. They each had different words written on their shirts. Some of them were POVERTY, HOPELESSNESS, HUSTLIN', ADDICTION, and LUST. They had their fists balled up and were glaring at a young man with a fire in his eyes. He had on baggy jeans and a wife beater. There was a beat up Bible in his back pocket, and a large silver crucifix swinging from his neck on a chain. Between him and the band of thugs there was an old man sitting at a table with a large open book. The young man stepped up to the table and leaned on it until he was looking the old man in the eyes. "You add my name to that list," he said with an unusual boldness. With a pen of golden ink, the old man wrote his name down in the book. "This is an ink that no one can erase," the old man said to him with a smile. "I know, sir," the young man said as he glanced at the thugs on the other side of the table, "and now I gotta go." Then the young man took off in a sprint running hard. He hit that pile of gangbangers like a lightening bolt. They were swinging and hitting at him as hard as they could, but he gave as good as he got. I saw that there was going to be no way they could hold him back. POVERTY grabbed him from behind and ADDICTION punched him three times in the stomach. But the young man struggled and shook himself free. He gave POVERTY such a hard punch to the throat that he never got up again. He swept ADDICTION'S legs right out from underneath him and then put him in a submission hold until ADDICTION started begging for mercy. LUST, HUSTLIN' and HOPELESSNESS saw their window to strike and they pounced on him like starving cats on a mouse. They were beating on him bad while he was finishing off ADDICTION. For a minute it looked like he might be done for. HOPELESSNESS, in particular, was dropping powerful blows as if he were trying to pound the young man into the ground like a railroad spike. But then with a great yell the young man tossed them off. He got back on his feet. With amazingly quick hands he fired punches into HUSTLIN' until he dropped to the pavement in a heap. HOPELESSNESS and LUST remained. HOPELESSNESS was built like a giant with arms like oil drums. LUST was small and shifty and he kept trying to sneak up behind the young man. The three of them circled around for a while with the young man in the middle. He had his guard up and though he was bruised and bleeding he wouldn't back down. Suddenly LUST shot in from behind with surprising quickness and gave him a savage punch in the side. The young man cried out but spun around and delivered a powerful kick that caused LUST to do a backflip. He was knocked out cold. Only HOPELESSNESS stood between the young man and the castle. "Better step off," the young man shouted. "You ain't so strong now that your friends are gone." HOPELESSNESS stood his ground. "I warned you, dawg," the young man said with a smile. Then he raced towards HOPELESSNESS like a running back who had just busted through the line with nothing but green grass ahead. HOPELESSNESS took one long hard swing, but he wasn't quick enough. The young man lit into him like a thunder crack, unleashing a combination of punches and kicks that were so powerful and so furious that HOPELESSNESS buckled up like a folding chair and fell to his knees. The young man put his hand on HOPELESS-NESS'S forehead, and then pushed the giant over as easy as if he were a balloon. With all of his enemies fallen, he took off running. He ran and ran until he came to the gate of the palace. He hollered at the top of his lungs, "I'm home, Master. Please take me in!" The large draw bridge came down and he hobbled in, totally exhausted. The door was pulled up again and I heard an explosion of cheers and clapping.

INTERPRETER: (with a nod) I think you know what this means, son.

KAI'RO: (grinning) Yeah. I know what this one is all about.

INTERPRETER: This walk that you've chosen is a beast, my son. Many many things will oppose you and try to destroy you. Some of them won't let up until you make it all the way. It's an everyday struggle, this walk you're on. You press on! Do you hear me?

KAI'RO: Yes sir. I hear you.

INTERPRETER: Let's look at one more room. I want you to meet Backslider and the Limping Saint.

STORYTELLER: They walked through a brown door into yet another room. There were two men miserably stuck in some nasty looking mud. They looked hopeless and helpless. Another man dressed in white came walking up to them. "Brothers," he said, "surely you don't want to remain in this mud all your lives. I can tell you how to get cleaned up and how to get your lives straightened up." He reached forward with a strong hand and pulled them out. They were then led to a small church where a pastor offered them a place to shower and clean up. When they came out, they were both cleaned up. Afterwards, the pastor read to them from his Bible about how they could be saved if they confessed their sins. Both men nodded that they wanted to do so. Then the man told them about the King and how He died for them and took the blame for all their nasty ways. He told them that they'd have to confess this King as Lord and give their lives over to Him. Both men bowed their heads and the pastor led them in a prayer. They asked that the King would forgive them, and said that they'd follow the King for the rest of their lives. They prayed for grace to change. They prayed that the King would help them change the sinful desires in their hearts and lives—the places where they had made mistakes and fallen into continual sin. As they asked for help, I saw that one guy was praying real hard. Tears were streaming down his face and he kept his head bowed toward the ground. The other guy was praying words, but he was just looking around and I could tell that he was just speaking to make *himself* feel better. When they were both done, the pastor gave them both a Bible and a hug. Then the two men walked out and took two different paths. One man fixed his eyes in his Bible as he walked down the path. Sometimes he'd fall down, but he always fell forward. And when he fell he got up quickly, dusted himself off, and then got going again. The further he walked and the more he read the less he fell, until he hardly fell at all. From some of his difficult and painful falls he started walking a little with a limp. But he never quit moving on.

The other man started walking on his path the same as the first guy, but it didn't take real long before he lost his Bible on the side of the road. He started falling too, but every time he fell he fell backwards. He took his time getting up, and before long the white robe the church gave him was getting real dirty and stained. Soon, he started stumbling and tripping more and more, and sometimes the falls were extremely painful. Finally, he took a really bad spill and tumbled backwards so far that he ended up back in that nasty mud where he started.

INTERPRETER: What do you see here?

KAI'RO: Well, it's obvious that Backslider is that dude that fell back in the mud again. And the Limpin' Saint is the dude that kept hobblin' down the road. That part is obvious, but why's he called Limpin' Saint?

INTERPRETER: We have to go back to the beginning of what we saw to understand. Both of those guys came from the same place. They were stuck in the mud of their sins. They heard the Good News and they both took an interest. But *interest* is as far as Backslider really took it. The Limping Saint heard the Good News and his soul burned for it. Even in the church when the pastor broke it down for them, Backslider just played along for a while because it sounded good to him and made him feel good to clean up for a while. Limpin' Saint took every word that the pastor shared very seriously, and he prayed that prayer with every part of who he was. When they left that church one of them left changed. Limpin' Saint discovered on the path that he wasn't perfect. *No one* is perfect. That is why he kept falling. But he learned that with the power of the Spirit in him, and the Bible in his hands, he had all that he needed to walk that path. He found the strength he needed to get up and keep going when he stumbled and fell.

KAI'RO: Yeah, but he always fell *forward*...

INTERPRETER: Exactly! That's the sign of a man making spiritual progress. A righteous man falls seven times but he keeps getting back up. A growing man *learns* from his mistakes. He prays for forgiveness and experiences the power to change and grow. Everyone walks the path with a limp because of indwelling sin and the damage from the times people give in to it. Sin will never be fully beaten on this side of heaven. We all have sin within us that still seeks to take control of our minds, our hearts, and our lives if we're not careful. So, a righteous man falls sometimes. But he keeps walking and learning. This is a sign of the King's grace in a man's life, and a sign that a man is growing in righteousness. A righteous man has no desire to stay down. He wants to see his life look more and more like the King's.

KAI'RO: Backslider always fell *backwards,* and he took some hard falls. Those looked painful.

INTERPRETER: His walk was like a man going off on a trip up a steep mountain with no shoes, no rope, no water or anything. He's able to get a little ways up the path with a lot of difficulty and scrapes, but after a while he's going to fall. Eventually he's going to be so weak he'll fall real hard and give up. Backslider didn't have the Spirit in him and he lost the only guidebook he had when he lost his Bible. The path of righteousness is not for people who are simply curious. It's for people who are unashamed and willing to go all the way. The King is faithful to give a man what he needs when He gives him His Spirit for strength and the light of His Word to show him the way.

STORYTELLER: The Interpreter took Kai'Ro down the hallway a little further until they came to another room with a door covered in many different colors.

INTERPRETER: This is a room with great truth.

STORYTELLER: He opened the door and I saw a large conference room with a big brown table. Seated at the middle of the table was a young man with a bright red T-shirt and a St. Louis cap on his head. He had his hands folded on the table and he looked angry. Then another young man walked into the room wearing a blue tall T-shirt and a throwback Milwaukee hat.

KAI'RO: Uh-oh. Something's about to go down here…

INTERPRETER: Keep watching, son.

STORYTELLER: The young man in blue sat down across from the kid in red and they glared at each other. Just then a white kid with a shaved head came in and sat two chairs down from the young man in red. From the tattoos on his arm and neck he looked like he was from a skinhead gang. A young and beautiful Hispanic girl came in from one end of the room and sat down and then a Middle-Eastern man with a long black beard did the same. An old Korean man entered followed by a well-dressed black woman in a business suit.

KAI'RO: This is crazy! What's happening here?

INTERPRETER: You will see soon.

STORYTELLER: A few Latino gangsters, a middle-aged white man in khaki shorts and a polo shirt, and a girl who looked like she was from Europe came in and sat down as well. Then suddenly the drama began. Several people stood up and started shouting and cursing. Several of them pointed at others around them and waved their arms in the air. The young man in red tossed his hat on the table and glared at the young man in blue across from him. He threw up some gang signs and the boy in blue threw up his. The white man in khakis shouted and cursed at the black woman in the business suit and she started screaming back at him. As those gathered around the table continued to snarl and threaten one another I noticed that there were several words spray painted on the Wall behind them. In dripping red paint were the words ADAM, IGNORANCE, RACISM, SEGREGATION, and also HATE. Then without warning several of the people in the room actually began to fight. There were punches thrown and even weapons pulled. It was a scary scene. Suddenly the projector on the ceiling kicked on and flashed a big picture of an Old Rugged Cross on the Wall behind them. Everyone stopped fighting and stared silently at the Cross. The picture remained there for one minute. Then with a loud crash like thunder the entire Wall fell down. For a moment no one could see because the room was filled with dust. As it began to clear, I could see a scene on the other side of the Wall. Everyone in the conference room had stopped to see what it was. It was an enormous room filled with millions and millions of people as far as my eye could see. There were people from all over the world with different colored skin and clothes, and they were speaking different languages. In the far distance at the opposite end of this room was a large throne and there was One seated on it. The light coming from this throne was blinding and I couldn't even look at it for long. Those in the conference room looked at each other and then back into the other room. Then the kid in the red shirt walked slowly over the crumbled bricks and into the other room. As he passed in, his red shirt and red hat were suddenly replaced by a bright white robe. He disappeared into the crowd already gathered inside. The kid in blue watched in amazement and then he followed, and the same thing happened. After he went, the others raced into the other room and they too became clothed in the amazingly bright white robes. Suddenly, everyone inside began to worship the One seated on the throne. It was the most beautiful sound I had ever heard.

KAI'RO: Wow. What does this mean...?

INTERPRETER: Well, what do you think?

KAI'RO: I don't know. I've never seen a room with so many mismatched kinds of people in it before. Whoever decided to bring all those people into that conference room must be a little crazy. There's no way all those different kinds a people are gonna get along all crammed in a small room like that...

INTERPRETER: The King called that meeting, son. You see so many people in the world hate other types of people because of all the things that they call 'differences.' It might be differences in skin color or differences in gender. Sometimes it's about what part of the world someone's from and sometimes it's something as small as what part of the block they're from. Some people hate others because of the differences in what they have in their bank accounts, and sometimes it's because of the differences in language. But really what causes people to hate each other, to develop racist feelings, and to live segregated lives is not the differences...it's actually what they all have in common.

KAI'RO: What do you mean?

INTERPRETER: What was the name that you saw on that Wall before it came crashing down?

KAI'RO: It was 'ADAM.'

INTERPRETER: That's right. You see, we've all got the same great-great-granddaddy in Adam. You have to go back to the beginning of time when sin first entered the world through Adam. He passed it on to each and every one of us. We're *all* sinners. There's no getting around it. All of the hatred in the world, the racism, and the segregation…these are *all* the foul fruit of sin. Sin has a million faces and every one of those faces seeks to divide us from God and to divide us from one another. Sin is a deadly disease that all of us have in common. It tears us all apart from really learning how to love one another.

KAI'RO: That's deep. So, the King's blood is the cure?

INTERPRETER: Yes. The common problem of sin is what keeps us all apart, but the common cure that can unite us all together is the blood of the King. The blood of the King destroys the work and the effects of sin. It builds a bridge between us and God, because apart from the King's saving grace we are enemies with God. It also tears down the walls that divide us from one another. When you give your life to the King things like race, gender, money, and what part of the block you grew up on no longer become your main form of identity. In that conference room everyone was divided from everyone else because of their sinful view of themselves and others around them. The thugs saw only their rag colors. Others could only see the differences in their skin. And they all hated people who didn't look the same. You saw some of those people showing hate because they didn't like others at the table who had more or less money than they did. All of them had put up sinful walls and barriers around themselves that didn't allow them to get to know one another.

KAI'RO: That's when the Cross came on the scene.

INTERPRETER: Exactly. Each of one of those folks gave their lives to the King. His blood became their new identity. It was like they were all adopted into a new family - the *same* family - with a new Father. They found unity in the King. The walls of race, gender, and different neighborhoods came crashing down and they were able to worship together as brothers and sisters. Those white robes that they all got were a sign of their unity in the King. The King's blood cleansed them and then His righteousness gave them a whole new outfit.

KAI'RO: That's too deep.

INTERPRETER: We sometimes forget that our worship on earth is supposed to imitate the worship going on in heaven. The Bible tells us that folks from every tribe, tongue, and nation are going to be worshipping the King in heaven. People from every background, every color, and every neighborhood are all going to be together doing the very same thing in heaven. Why can't we try to bring a little of that here to earth?

KAI'RO: That's powerful. I think this earth could use a 'lil more heaven these days.

INTERPRETER: (smiling) Yes it could, my son. Now let's go have a look at that painting that struck you, and then I will see you on your way.

STORYTELLER: The two went back out into the main hallway again until they stopped in front of the big painting. It was picture of two different scenes. In one scene was a young man who looked a lot like Kai'Ro. The young man was on his knees in front of a large wooden cross. His head was bowed and his hands were folded. Behind him was a pile of things. There was a big stack of cash, a bunch of trophies that the young man had won, a fancy looking Benz, a shiny magazine with his face on the front, and a black gun. When Kai'Ro saw the gun he swallowed hard and looked at the Interpreter, but the Interpreter didn't notice. Behind the pile of things was a group of people. There was a beautiful young woman that looked like she might have been Kai'Ro's girl, and there were some other guys that looked like they were probably his boys. There was an older looking woman that looked a lot like his mama and she was standing next to another young man that looked like his brother. All of them stood away from him at a distance.

KAI'RO: I think I got this side of the picture. That guy is sayin' goodbye to everything the world has to offer. It's like he knows that the Cross has everything he needs and he's turned his back on everything else...looks like he even said goodbye to his family. These losses are *hard.*

INTERPRETER: That's right. The King on that Cross must become your treasure and everything else should be trash in comparison.

KAI'RO: But what about this side of the picture? What does it mean?

STORYTELLER: On the other side of the picture the young man in the painting was on his feet again. He had stepped over the pile of things and he had his arms wide open as if he was trying real hard to tell the group of people behind him something real important. Most of the others had their backs turned towards him and some were even walking away with their fingers in their ears. A few of them stuck around. I noticed that one of them was the boy who looked like his brother. The kid had a look on his face like he was really listening and thinking.

INTERPRETER: (looking at Kai'Ro) Son, once you find yourself at the Cross, the Master is going to call you to go back...

KAI'RO: (raising his voice) Back to the City of Doom?

INTERPRETER: Maybe. I can't really say. Going back sometimes means going back to where you came from. Sometimes it doesn't. Either way you're going to receive your marching orders.

KAI'RO: I don't get it.

INTERPRETER: You won't fully get this until you meet the Arms Dealer. There you'll receive your weapons and you'll also receive your marching orders.

KAI'RO: *Marching* orders?

INTERPRETER: It's as I said. Later, you'll understand more clearly. Now, son, it's time for you to get going. You are about to make the most important decision of your life.

KAI'RO: I'm ready. Thanks for your time, sir. I learned a lot here today.

INTERPRETER: There is much more to learn, son. You are just beginning. Keep your mind open to knowledge and your heart open to wisdom, and the King will give it to you.

STORYTELLER: The two of them walked to the front door. Kai'Ro thanked the Interpreter, shook his hand, and took off back onto the Heavenly Highway.

CHAPTER SIX:
BIRDVILLE

STORYTELLER: After leaving the Interpreters house Kai'Ro came quickly upon a town called Birdville. There was a black and yellow flag flapping from a pole with a picture of three large birds gobbling up a bunch of scattered seeds on the ground. Just beyond the town he could see a hill and on top of the hill a wooden cross. He took a deep breath and entered the town after he understood that it was the only way to the hill. There were a bunch of stores on either side with names like the "Confused Coffee Shop" and "Happy Living Bookstore." In the windows of the stores were blurry posters advertising things that Kai'Ro couldn't understand. A few men and women moved along the sidewalk but they hardly looked at him as he moved past them. He stopped for a minute because everyone was wearing the same kind of strange black slim-rimmed glasses. I could see that Kai'Ro was growing concerned. He noticed some more places with names like "Love My Body Gym" and "Mo Money School of Wild Living." There were lots of people moving in and out of the stores. At the very center of town was a huge factory that had big puffs of grey smoke coming out of the dirty stacks. The factory was called "Clouded Vision Eye Glasses." There were rows and rows of eighteen-wheelers in the main parking lot, and several trucks left the factory and rumbled past Kai'Ro down the street. On the side of the factory was the same logo I saw on the flag with the birds and seeds. Across the street from the factory was a nice hotel called "Pilgrim Trap". The flashy sign said: " Vacancy."

KAI'RO: (speaking to himself) What kinda' place *is this*? Why is this town right here at the foot of the Cross?

STORYTELLER: Just then a tall man in a dark black suit came out of a tinted office complex next to the factory, and spotting Kai'Ro, he hollered at him. He had on the same pair of glasses as everyone else.

MAN: Where you going, son? You aren't about to go up that mountain there are you?

KAI'RO: That's why I'm here. Who're you?

MAN: I'm Blindman. This is my factory. I saw you through the window and had to come out and stop you.

KAI'RO: What'cha mean, stop me? I've already come this far. I don't think you can stop me.

BLINDMAN: Don't be foolish, son. That whole trip up there isn't necessary. So many people think it is, but it isn't. Look around you. We've got ourselves a thriving town here in Birdville. This town was founded a long time ago to spare people the trouble of going up that mountain and getting disappointed. Besides look at the path up that mountain. It's almost impossible.

STORYTELLER: I looked at the mountain as Kai'Ro took a look himself. There was a very noticeable path that was steep but it was clearly a path that anyone could climb up if they really wanted to.

KAI'RO: I don't get it…

BLINDMAN: Look at that hill you're about to climb. Have you ever tried to climb something so dangerous before?

KAI'RO: (looking up at the hill) First of all, man, it doesn't look that steep or dangerous to me. Besides that, I can see the Cross up there at the top right now. It looks amazin'. I'm sure you can see that.

BLINDMAN: No, sorry son. I don't see anything except a ridiculously tall hill.

KAI'RO: I don't understand…

BLINDMAN: Exactly. That's what we're here to do. That's what I'm here to do, son. I'm here to provide you with some understanding and some clear sight. Whoever told you to go up there has filled your head with a bunch of nonsense. Look at me. You don't need to do it, son. There is nothing ahead of you but a long hard journey filled with frustration.

KAI'RO: I don't think you understand. I've got a real burden on my back. It's a burden of sin and a guilty conscience. I'm gonna go up there and get rid of it.

BLINDMAN: (with a stern face) I'm older than you, young man, and I've been here a long, long time. I know more than you. Who are you to talk to me about understanding? That burden has nothing to do with sin and a guilty conscience. It has everything to do with a troubled mind because someone put some thoughts in there that made you feel bad about yourself. Look around you for a minute. Do you see anyone who looks guilty or even troubled?

STORYTELLER: Kai'Ro took a moment to look at some of the people walking the streets. No one looked that bothered. They just moved around from store to store and place to place like any normal person would. He turned back to Blindman and shrugged his shoulders.

BLINDMAN: Son, you don't see correctly yet. Once you see you'll understand. You need a pair of these glasses. I should have a pair right here.

STORYTELLER: Blindman reached into his pockets and seemed to get real frustrated when he couldn't find a pair.

BLINDMAN: Tell you what, son. See the Pure Sight Vision Center over there across the street? I'll take you there myself and we'll get you what you need. You'll see a lot better after that. Here, I'll go with you. We'll get you the exact pair.

STORYTELLER: Kai'Ro looked at where the man was pointing and saw the *Clouded* Vision Center. He looked confused.

KAI'RO: Man, you pointin' to the *Clouded* Vision Center over there, 'cause I don't see no *Pure* Sight Vision Center.

BLINDMAN: It's right there, son. Look!

KAI'RO: Yeah, I'm lookin' right there. That doesn't say Pure Sight Vision Center…

BLINDMAN: Wow, your sight is worse than I thought. The vision center is right next to the Holy Living Bookstore right there.

KAI'RO: You mean the *Happy* Living Bookstore?

BLINDMAN: Okay, boy, now you're just being hardheaded. I've been in Birdville all my life and I've hardly met anyone with a problem as bad as yours.

KAI'RO: (raising his eyebrow) Look, man. I don't know what kind of joke you're tryin' to play on me, but it ain't funny. You're accusin' me of bein' blind and hardheaded. I know I can read, man! Quit playin'.

BLINDMAN: Son, do you see all of these trucks leaving the factory here? I have hundreds of trucks pull out of here every day delivering these glasses and giving sight to people all over the world. There's a lot of people that just don't understand at all. People just like you. Providing people with sight is a legitimate business. This town has been giving people sight longer than anyone can really remember. The only joke in town is *you*, boy!

STORYTELLER: Just then Blindman had a determined look appear on his face. He pulled his glasses off and he handed them to Kai'Ro.

BLINDMAN: Here, try these on. You'll see what I mean when you try these on. Go ahead. Put them on and then take a look at that hill you're headed for.

STORYTELLER: Kai'Ro appeared doubtful, but he decided to give them a try. Cautiously, he put them on and turned to look at the hill. He looked shocked.

KAI'RO: Man, *where's* the Cross? Where's the Cross?! I don't see nothin'! Where'd it go? Man, what's goin' on here?

STORYTELLER: Kai'Ro ripped the glasses off his face and shoved them back into Blindman's hands.

KAI'RO: Those glasses are evil, dawg! Don't get those things near me! I couldn't see a thing with those glasses on. They made the Cross disappear. This whole town is an evil place. I need to get out of here *now*!

STORYTELLER: As Kai'Ro was shouting, some of the other people stopped to see what was going on. Some of them closed in around him.

BLINDMAN: Son, you need to calm down. You've got some serious problems and we can help you if you'll just let us. If you let us help you see then you'll understand…

KAI'RO: Naw, man, *you* need the help. *All ya'll need some help.* Can't you see that you're all blind. Don't you understand what I'm sayin'? Ya'll have been robbed of your sight and your understanding. You need to get rid of those glasses, man, for real. Those things are so messed up! Someone needs to shut that factory down! Look what you're doin' to everybody. None of these people can see! You've got 'em all fooled.

(To the crowd) Don't ya'll get it that these glasses have robbed you of understanding? You live in a town right here by the Cross and yet none of ya'll can even see how close to salvation you actually are! Don't ya care? This man and these glasses are blindin' you! Take those doggone things off your face and come with me.

BLINDMAN: (angrily) You don't understand, do you, son? Those glasses give all of us the ability to see. There's nothing messed up in this town but your eyes! You can't see! That's why I'm trying so hard to get you to the vision center. Once you own a pair of these glasses it will all make sense, you'll understand that you're wrong and that you can finally see. Most everyone here was sort of like you at one point. Stop any one of these people and ask them how they feel. They'll tell you that they feel wonderful.

KAI'RO: No. I'm not talkin' to no one no more. This place is crazy. I'm headin' up that hill and leavin' this place behind forever.

STORYTELLER: Kai'Ro turned and ran as fast as he could down the street leaving Blindman and the others behind. He ran hard and he never looked back.

CHAPTER SEVEN:
THE MOUNTAIN
AND THE CROSS

STORYTELLER: As Kai'Ro moved away from the city and towards the hill he discovered that the path was protected on both sides by a wall. The wall was called SALVATION. From far away the hill looked a lot like a mountain, but up close it seemed a lot smaller. Kai'Ro came to the bottom of the hill and stopped to look at an old wooden sign that read, "Come to me, all who labor and are heavy burdened, and I will give you rest." I could see tears forming in Kai'Ro's eyes as he read that sign, and I could also see that he was struggling under the weight of the burden.

KAI'RO: (to himself) C'mon! You can do this thing. The hope for your soul is at that Cross. All the pain, guilt, and drama ends there. All the peace, relief, and life begins there.

STORYTELLER: He started to climb up the hill running at first, but his burden made it hard for him. He stumbled a couple of times, but he kept getting up. I could tell that he was desperate. The burden got heavier as he drew closer to the Cross. It weighed down on him like a boulder. He dropped to his knees and the burden started to pull him backward.

KAI'RO: This burden is going to crush me! I don't think I can make it to the top. All my sins…they're just too much…I don't even know if the Cross is strong enough to break the bonds of this burden…I don't know if the King can really take away all the mess and mistakes in my life. They're just too nasty and too foul.

STORYTELLER: Kai'Ro started crawling like a desperate man groping through a desert in search of water. For a moment it looked like he could go no further. His arms and legs were shaking under all the weight. His head was bowed because the power of the burden left him broken and nearly hopeless. Then, just as he came to a point where he could go no further, I saw two small birds land on his shoulder. On one of the bird's wings was the word GRACE and on the other bird was the word REDEMPTION. These two birds gently started to peck away at the straps holding his burden. One of the straps eventually snapped with a loud crack. As it did, I saw a shiver of renewed life return to Kai'Ro's body. I saw strength come to his limbs. He was able to slowly rise to his feet again and continue on. To the side of the path was an open grave. Kai'Ro looked at it for a minute but just kept going. Past the open grave Kai'Ro saw an old wooden Cross and as he did the burden on his back tumbled off, bounced down the path, fell into the open grave and then disappeared from sight. Kai'Ro fell on his knees at the foot of the Cross and his shoulders were shaking because he was crying so hard. Just then three visitors who looked like angels appeared and placed their hands upon him.

VISITOR ONE: Rise to your feet Kai'Ro. You are a new creation. The old has gone and the new has come. You do not need to be ashamed for your King is not ashamed. He welcomes you to His City of Gold, and He adopts you as His son.

VISITOR TWO: Clothe yourself in righteousness.

STORYTELLER: The second visitor took away Kai'Ro's dirty rags and gave him a fresh white tall-t and some clean jeans and tennis shoes. The third visitor put a mark of oil on his right cheek and handed him a small scroll that was tied together with a golden seal.

VISITOR THREE: Take this scroll and give it to he who guards the gate at the City of Gold and he will bid you welcome.

VISITOR ONE: Do you know what your name means son?

KAI'RO: My mom never really said…

VISITOR TWO: It's an ancient name with tremendous historical significance. From the early days of the church the Chi-Rho was a symbol for the follower of the King. In fact, it was really a symbol for the King Himself.

KAI'RO: What'cha mean?

VISITOR THREE: The ancient Greek letter "chi" and the letter "rho" were the first two letters to the King's name, *Christos*. The early church believers combined those first two letters into the unique symbol "☧". This is the symbol that I have placed on your face. It is a mark for you to go by as a follower of the King. But it is also *your name.*

KAI'RO: I guess my mom kinda blessed me with a name that would fulfill my destiny or something.

VISITOR ONE: The King had your destiny laid out from the beginning of time, my child. Your name is special and now you must learn in obedience to walk in it.

STORYTELLER: As quickly as they came they disappeared. Kai'Ro was left alone at the top of the hill. His face was full of joy. He tucked the scroll into his back pocket and started back down the other side of the hill. As he came to the bottom two guys jumped over the wall along the side of the path. They both looked surprised to see Kai'Ro.

KAI'RO: Yo, where'd you two come from?

E.Z. GLIDE: Me and my man, 2-Face came from the town of Prideopolis. We're on our way to the City of Gold.

KAI'RO: Yeah? You skipped the Gate, dawg. You can't just jump the wall like that.

2-FACE: Look, for those of us in Prideopolis, it's too far to backtrack like that and go through the Gate. You took your way through the Gate, and we took ours by hopping over the wall. What's the big deal?

KAI'RO: The King said that guys like you are thieves who come sneakin' over the fence and that ain't gonna work.

E.Z. GLIDE: You don't need to worry about us, playa! We've got our thing figured out fo sho! Looks like you got on some slick clean t-shirt that somebody probably gave you to cover up you being naked or somethin! What's that all about?

KAI'RO: This clean clothes was given to me by the The King of the Place where I'm goin! Yeah, it's to cover my nakedness, and I'm thankful for this clothes. Where's your scroll? Where's your proof that you came by the way of the Cross, dude? You got nothin' to prove that you're for real. You two are going to be turned away. You need to go by the way of the Gate. There is no other way.

2-FACE: (laughing) Look, dawg, I don't even know you. You got your little religious spin and everything, and that's cool for you, but we got our plan too.

KAI'RO: I'm not playin'. You two are foolin' yourselves big time. I came in under the King's directions, but you two came on this Highway followin' your own dreams and when you get there you're going to get turned away without His mercy.

E.Z. GLIDE: Look, man, we're on the same Way as you, and we follow the Law and the Customs of the King real good. Probably even *better* than you. I don't think you get it, homie.

KAI'RO: Following the Law and Customs of the King is a good thing, but that ain't going to save you in the end. You gotta come by the Gate. How many more times do I have to say that, dude? My King is going to recognize me because I got His clothes on, and I got His mark on me, and I got his scroll in my pocket, and that doggone burden I've had all my life fell tumblin' off at the foot of the Cross. I'm the King's son for real now.

STORYTELLER: E.Z. Glide and 2-Face burst into laughter and pointed at Kai'Ro. The two of them walked on with Kai'Ro ahead just a few steps. From time to time the two would point at Kai'Ro and crack on him. He never said anything other than muttering a few things to encourage himself. Eventually, they came to a hill called DIFFICULTY. There was a refreshing stream of cold water in front of the hill and two easier paths going around the hill. Kai'Ro sat down to get a drink from the cold waters, but the other two dudes split up, each to take a different road. They thought that their paths would cross again on the other side of the tall hill, DIFFICULTY. 2-Face took a path called DESPAIR which disappeared into a dark and dense woods. EZ-Glide took a path called DESTRUCTION which went into some deep mountains. In those mountains he took a hard fall and couldn't get up again. No one would be able to find him. Kai'Ro went on his way straight up DIFFICULTY. It was a struggle. He started off strong, but after a while he had to stoop over and use his hands because the hill was so steep. About half way up he was tired and breathing real hard. There was a little shelter for rest. It had a roof that gave travelers like him some shade.

KAI'RO: (to himself) This looks like a good place to chill for a minute. I'm so tired. Maybe I could just lay down for a second or two...

STORYTELLER: Kai'Ro leaned up against one of the poles that supported the roof and he fell asleep real fast. He was there for a while resting and snoring. Then all of a sudden he woke up with a jump.

KAI'RO: (to himself) Aw, man, the desire of the sluggard kills him, for his hands refuse to labor!

STORYTELLER: Kai'Ro got up and was very mad at himself. The sun had started to dip in the sky. He knew he had wasted too much time.

KAI'RO: I'm supposed to run with endurance this race that's been marked out for me. I'm a fool! I been sleepin' in the shade when I should be on my way. Can't believe I did that...

STORYTELLER: He continued to climb hard for quite a while until he was almost to the top. He reached into his back pocket because he wanted to look at his scroll for some encouragement, but he suddenly realized that it was gone. He was so mad and so scared that he almost started crying. He looked to his left and then he looked to his right. He checked all of his pockets.

KAI'RO: (to himself) Kai'Ro, you been foolish, now you've lost the most important thing you've got. If you've messed up this bad this early in your trip, how are you ever gonna finish this thing?

STORYTELLER: There was still a little light left on the path and so Kai'Ro took off back down the hill again looking everywhere along the path. The further back he went the madder he got at himself until he was almost tempted to start cursing again. The scroll was no where to be found. After a while he made it back to the covered rest area where he fell asleep. It was almost too dark to see and so he got down on his hands and knees reaching around on the ground for his scroll.

KAI'RO: Man, if I lost it, then what am I goin' to do? God, please let me find this thing...

STORYTELLER: Just when he was about to lose all hope his hand fell on his scroll. He jumped up and shouted! Kai'Ro was overjoyed that he had found his scroll and he took off back up the hill with new strength and purpose. He made it to the top again in half the time it took him earlier. At the top of the hill there was level ground again. A short way down the path he could see the lights of a town. Now that it was dark he was encouraged thinking to himself that he could find a place to sleep for the night. He hurried quickly until he came to the edge of the town. He read a sign along the side of the road that said: Rock City: Suffer No Longer.

KAI'RO: (to himself) What kinda place is *this*?

STORYTELLER: Kai'Ro looked unsure about this city, but there were lights down the main street which was called Fall Away Avenue. There were a few people hanging out in front of a restaurant. They watched Kai'Ro as he started passing by.

KAI'RO: How's it goin'?

TURNBACK JACK: It's good. Where you headin' to?

KAI'RO: I'm on my way to the City of Gold.

TJ: Well, you might as well park it here, homie. You don't want to go up that way any further.

KAI'RO: Yeah? Why's that?

SHIFTY: There's danger up that way. There's all kinds of hard things down that road.

KAI'RO: Everyone knows that. That doesn't mean I'm gonna stop here. I'm headin' on to the City of Gold. There's no way I'm goin' lose my burden and then just call it quits like that.

TJ: I had the same thoughts 'bout a year ago. I was headin' up that way, but there's a big 'ole house not too far down the path and they got these two crazy big red-nosed pits there, dawg. They're right up on the path and there was no way I was goin' risk that. Not for real.

KAI'RO: The King promised anyone who followed after Him that there'd be trials and suffering.   I mean, I think everybody knows that.

SHIFTY: We'll see. I never even made it to the big house like Turn-back Jack here. I got just a ways down the road and there was a bunch of dudes that clowned on me so bad. They made fun of my clothes, my mark and everything. I tried to talk to them a little but then they got loud and one of them boys even slapped me. I was thinkin' to myself, 'Naw, I didn't sign up to get slapped around like that.' So, I headed back and moved to Rock City. There's a lot of folks here that found this place to be a lot safer. We still believe in the King and everything, but we ain't really interested in walkin' down that road of suffering…

KAI'RO: But the King said that if we weren't willin' to pick up our cross and follow after Him then there was no point in even botherin' with Him. I don't think you can really say you believe in Him if you ain't willin' to follow after Him.

TJ: Man, look here. I've had enough drama in my life. I grew up in a bad home with a no good dad and and a deadbeat moms. I grew up on the streets and lived the street life. You feel me? I decided to believe in the King to leave all that drama behind. I didn't decide to believe in Him so that I could have more drama. You crazy? Shoot! Rock City is where it's at. We left the nonsense behind and we ain't goin' to find no more nonsense either.

SHIFTY: We'll wait right here doin' our thing until the King comes back like He said He would. He'll find us here and it'll all be straight.

KAI'RO: I don't think ya'll get it. You don't understand for real. I had drama in my life too, and I left it behind in order to lose the burden of my sin. But the King didn't just want to make me feel better. Trust me, man, I feel better than I've ever felt in my life, but He also told me to follow after Him, and that's what I'm doing come hell or whatever. It don't matter. I'm in this thing till the end.

TJ: Then go for it, dawg. When you see those pits you'll be runnin' back here just like about how everybody else does. We ain't here to clown on you, man. We're just trying to let you know that Rock City is where it's at, and you don't have to head down a road full of thugs, beasts, and suffering.

KAI'RO: I'm not coming back through here, and I hope that my courage will inspire some of ya'll to follow after me. You're wastin' your life dropping out of the race like ya'll doing. You're goin' to find yourselves disqualified at the end and it'll be sad. Ya'll need to bounce out this joint and come with me…

TJ: You won't be coming back…not because you made it somewhere further but because you'll be dead. There've been a few cats who made it past the pits some how but they came back all scared talkin' about demons, persecutions, and one dude even said there's a whole city out there where they actually thrash followers of the King's and put some of 'em to death. No thanks, dude. I'm waitin' right here.

KAI'RO: Then you wait for nothin', man, because no one's comin' for you. When the King comes back your lamps will be out of oil and you'll miss Him. I wish you'd listen to me and come with me.

SHIFTY: There was another guy like you who passed through here earlier this morning. He wouldn't listen to us either. Maybe you'll find him or what's left of him up there if you hurry.

KAI'RO: For real? Then I'm out…

CHAPTER EIGHT:
THE ARMS
DEALER

STORYTELLER: Kai'Ro said bye to Turnback Jack and Shifty and moved quickly through what was left of Rock City. He was glad to leave such a pathetic place behind. The words about the pits scared him some. It was dark and he knew he'd have no chance against them. He moved on for awhile until he saw a big flashing sign along the side of the road. The sign said: "Thorn Town," and it had a bright gold arrow pointing to a side path. On the sign there were pictures of pimped out cars with chrome wheels, gorgeous looking girls, and mountains of cash. Kai'Ro stopped to stare at it for a while. He read the slogan at the bottom: *Fame and Fortune Just Around the Corner*. He said to himself, "Don't store up treasure for yourself where moth and rust destroy and where thieves break in and steal." He pulled out his scroll and read. The Spirit of the King gripped him and gave him strength. He moved on. A short ways down the path he found a large house just like the guys in Rock City had told him. He moved close to the door until he heard a loud barking. In the path just ahead of the house he saw the two huge pit bulls. They were much larger than normal and almost looked like mutants. One had a large tag that said Lockjaw on it and the other was named Bonecruncher. He started shaking. He didn't know if they had seen him yet.

KAI'RO: (to himself) Aw, shoot! Those dogs are right in my way. There's no where to go. I either gotta try to sneak up there, or I gotta go back and face those guys again.

STORYTELLER: Kai'Ro stood there for a while just trembling in the shadows. He looked terrible. He took two steps forward and then one step backward like he couldn't make up his mind. Just then someone opened up a window at the top of the house and saw him.

KEEPER: Hey down there! What are you doing?

KAI'RO: I'm makin' my way down the Heavenly Highway, but there's two pits out here that won't let me go any further.

KEEPER: Don't worry about those dogs, boy. They're on chains and they can't reach you if you stay to the middle of the path.

KAI'RO: For real? I dunno, man.

KEEPER: Trust me. Stick to the path. Come here and you can stay here tonight. It's no good for you to be out on the Highway in the dark.

STORYTELLER: Kai'Ro took a few careful steps forward until the pits were so close that he could feel them breathing. From the light of the house he could see that they were both chained up like the man in the house had said. He was encouraged and walked quickly up to the door. One of the pits growled again and Kai'Ro jumped up on the porch and started beating on the door.

KEEPER: (opening the door a crack) Where are you from?

KAI'RO: I'm Kai'Ro from the City of Doom.

KEEPER: And how'd you get here?

KAI'RO: I came through the Gate, and just this morning made it to Mountain of the Cross. I lost my burden there. Just a few minutes ago I went through Rock City back there…

KEEPER: You sound like you are a true pilgrim. Come in.

STORYTELLER: Kai'Ro stepped into the house. He was relieved to be in a warm place and away from the dogs.

KEEPER: We're just about to have dinner. You're welcome to join me and the girls.

KAI'RO: Girls?

KEEPER: Yes. My two daughters, Purity and Peaceful.

STORYTELLER: The Keeper led him into a large dining room. There were two beautiful young girls setting the table. They were dressed nicely in long colorful dresses and they looked at Kai'Ro with kind smiles.

PURITY: Hello. Will you be joining us for dinner?

KAI'RO: If I can, I'd love to eat with ya'll.

PURITY: Are you a pilgrim on the King's Highway?

KAI'RO: Yeah. I am.

PEACEFUL: Then please sit down and tell us about your journey so far.

STORYTELLER: The four of them sat down to some delicious food. The girls had cooked fried chicken, collards, potatoes, and macaroni and cheese. Kai'Ro told them all about his City of Doom. He explained to them how he met the Preacher and how the Preacher explained the problem of sin to him. Kai'Ro discussed how he left with Follower and Quitter and how they abandoned him at the Swamp of Despair. He shared with them his conversations with Goodwill, in Birdville, and with many of the travelers he met on the way. They listened to him for a long time without interrupting. When he finished one of the girls spoke to him.

PURITY: Did you have a wife back in your city?

KAI'RO: No. I mean I wanted to marry my girl, Evangeline. We just hadn't done it yet.

PEACEFUL: Didn't you tell her about the Heavenly Highway?

KAI'RO: We talked about it a lot. She'd always just laugh and tell me that I was gettin' religious on her.

PURITY: Did you feel like your new passion for the Heavenly Highway affected your relationship?

KAI'RO: Yeah. I loved Evangeline so much, but I started feelin' like our relationship was wrong. I couldn't keep livin' with her like we were doin'.

PEACEFUL: And did you tell her that?

KAI'RO: Yeah, I told her. She got mad. She couldn't understand it. It was like we were on two different planets or something. I begged her to listen to what was goin' on in my heart, but she just said she didn't feel what I was feelin'.

PURITY: Didn't you tell her about sin and that sin would destroy her if she wasn't willing to change?

KAI'RO: I told her that sin would destroy us both. I even told her that our sin would kill our relationship eventually, but she just got madder and madder. She said that I was judgin' her and she told me I was in no place to be her judge. I told her that God was our judge and that we'd broken all His laws and that we were in terrible trouble unless we made some real changes. I explained to her that we had to get on that Heavenly Highway and that the King would give us grace and forgive us for what we'd done. When I said that she just stared at me and didn't say nothin'. I knew then that I'd have to go without her. So that's what I've done.

PEACEFUL: You have made a very hard decision, but you've made a good one. As the King said, you must hate your father and your mother in comparison to your love for Him or you can't be His disciple. You have chosen life and your decision will not leave her unchanged if she truly loves you as it sounds like she does. We must pray that she will follow after you.

KAI'RO: I pray it every day.

KEEPER: Thank you for sharing your story with us, son. You have taken bold steps that most people are unwilling to make. A beautiful girl, a stack of cash, or any flashy thing can keep a man or woman from following the King. Tell me something, did you come by Thorn Town?

KAI'RO: I saw the sign. The sign was tight, I'm not gonna lie.

KEEPER: Well, it's good that you did not visit. Many travelers toss in their towel there.

KAI'RO: Why's that?

KEEPER: Thorn Town is a place that makes a lot of promises. People go there in search of fame, fortune, and all kinds of pleasure. For a while the town gives what it promises. They've got girls there, a lot of ways to make quick cash, and some people go there and they actually make it big. But like a thorny weed the town chokes the life out of people. Whatever passion and hope they found at the Cross they exchange for the goods of the city. It's like the hope of the City of Gold just gets strangled and dies. It is one of Diablo's greatest cities and one of his greatest traps. Few go there and come back because it has an evil power to it. There are few things more destructive to the soul than a strong love for the pleasures and power of this world.

KAI'RO: I feel you. I'm glad I pressed on.

KEEPER: As are we. Tomorrow morning I will take you to the Arms Dealer. He will give you what you need for the remainder of this journey.

KAI'RO: Like what?

KEEPER: All of the King's travelers need to get armed for the battles ahead. There will be many and without the armor you could easily be overcome.

KAI'RO: Well, I'm up for any help that I can get on this trip. Did another guy pass this way? Some of the cats back in Rock City said a guy went through there this morning. After what you said, I hope he didn't stop off at Thorn Town.

KEEPER: Yes, a man named Phanatik came by around noon today. He ate with us and then stopped off at the Arms Dealer. This is a very special man. I hope that you can catch him tomorrow.

KAI'RO: Did you say, Phanatik? I know him. He's from my city! This is great news. I'm goin' to have to bust it tomorrow if I'm goin' to catch him.

KEEPER: I pray that you overtake him. Come with me and I'll show you your room.

STORYTELLER: Kai'Ro went to his room and slept hard after his long day. He woke up the next morning feeling strong and ready to go. After a short breakfast he followed the Keeper down the path to a stone house with two long swords mounted above the door. The Keeper knocked on the door and a huge man answered it. He had a bright white wife beater on and his arms were nearly as big as Kai'Ro's waist. Kai'Ro just stood there and stared.

ARMS DEALER: Well, what we got here, Keeper? He 'nother traveler?

KEEPER: Yes. This is Kai'Ro from the City of Doom. He's in need of some armor.

ARMS DEALER: Well, then, he's in the right place ain't he? Come on in.

KAI'RO: Don't you hate guys like me?

ARMS DEALER: Huh? Ohh…you must be referrin' to this tattoo I got on my arm here…Yeah, I used to hate guys like you. Fact is…I used to hate a lot of folks. Not no more though. This tattoo is a symbol from my past and a part of me that I ain't too proud of. When I gave my life to the King He took all that hate just right outta me, man. The art on my arm is kinda like a scar of who I once was, but I ain't like that no more. The King made me a new man. When I get my new body in glory the tattoo'll be gone for good. I want you to know that I got no ill feelins' towards you or nothin'.

KAI'RO: Guess we all kinda got scars from our past.

STORYTELLER: Kai'Ro went into the house. It was much bigger than he imagined. There were armor, helmets, shields, and swords everywhere. There were so many that it looked like he could give armor to everyone in the world if they wanted it. There were big fires going and the Arms Dealer was obviously making more.

ARMS DEALER: Come over here and I'll git you what you need. But before I git you set up, you need to give me a little somethin' don't you?

STORYTELLER: The Arms Dealer smiled and winked at Kai'Ro.

KAI'RO: What'cha mean?

ARMS DEALER: Now that you're a part of the King's army you'll be doing battle in a different kinda way. Yer weapons from the City of Doom ain't no good in this battle.

STORYTELLER: Kai'Ro suddenly looked a little embarrassed. He took off his backpack and unzipped it. He pulled out his shiny black gun and handed it to the Arms Dealer.

KAI'RO: That thing got me out of a lot of jams back where I came from.

ARMS DEALER: The weapons of the world are for killin'. Yer no longer in a fight 'gainst flesh and blood, but 'gainst much darker and more powerful enemies. Guns and bullets ain't gonna do nothing 'gainst them.

KAI'RO: What'cha mean? I've never seen anyone that can stop a bullet.

ARMS DEALER: That may be true, but you'll be fightin' against the forces of Hell now. They ain't 'fraid of bullets, bombs, or the weapons of this world. They yield only to the Sword.

STORYTELLER: The Arms Dealer handed Kai'Ro a small but very sharp sword.

KAI'RO: Shoot, this thing is tiny! You sure I can do some damage with this?

ARMS DEALER: Don't you worry 'bout the size of the blade in your hand, friend.. This Sword is not made for tearing stuff up. It's the weapon of a skilled warrior that is thrust forward only once to deal a deadly blow. It's an assassin's blade. Your other weapons are made to protect your heart and soul from destruction.

STORYTELLER: The Arms Dealer placed a helmet on Kai'Ro's head, a breastplate on his chest, some crazy looking shoes on his feet, and then he handed him a light shield.

KAI'RO: I feel kinda foolish wearin' this stuff. I mean, nobody wears this kinda stuff.

ARMS DEALER: The King's armor has stood out since the beginning of time. There's nothin' like it and anyone who sees it knows that the one who wears it and uses it belongs to the King. But the armor ain't heavy and clunky. It's light so you can move quick, but it's strong to keep you safe…

STORYTELLER: Kai'Ro looked himself over as if he was trying to figure out how he felt about everything.

KAI'RO: So why's all the armor have 116 on it?

ARMS DEALER: It's a reminder from the King's Word. It reminds the wearer of the armor that there ain't no shame in the Gospel. Any man or woman who wears this armor must go into battle and into every town unashamed. You must also be willing to face any friend or foe with the power of the Gospel.

KAI'RO: I can feel that.

ARMS DEALER: You are now an ambassador for the King. Yer an agent of reconciliation to a dying world. Yer equipped to do battle with the powers of Hell. You now have heavenly weapons that can destroy strongholds. When you must fight, do everything you can to stand. As a good soldier don't get yerself tangled up in the treasure and traps of this world. Use the Shield of the Faith to protect yerself 'gainst the blows of the enemy when he strikes to crush you. Let the Helmet of Salvation remind you always that yer saved and that you belong to the King. The Breastplate of Righteousness will guard yer heart and keep it secure. The Shoes on yer feet are the Shoes of Prayer. Sometimes you'll face enemies that ain't gonna back down to the Sword n' so you must keep goin' forward in prayer. Pray for yerself, pray for the King's Kingdom to go forth, and pray for all of yer fellow soldiers. You hear what I'm sayin'?

KAI'RO: Yeah, I feel you.

ARMS DEALER: Remember that this battle is 24/7. There ain't *no breaks* from this fight. Don't fall back and don't get lazy. Some folks will tuck and run when the heat gets turned up. Some will get bored, others captured, 'n a few may even become traitors like that boy, Demas. Stand yer ground and the King will always provide you with what you need. Those who fight the good fight are more than conquerers. Even their enemies become their slaves. The armor is yours to wear day and night. Never take it off or forget about it or you may get thrashed. It will guard you and keep you effective in our struggle for the King's Kingdom. I gotta tell you that you will prob'ly suffer, you will hurt, n' you may even die in this battle here. But, rejoice that you can bear the wounds n' scars of yer King, for your reward is great in His Kingdom. The harder you fight the more yer soul will blaze with fire and the more yer joy will grow. There is no greater calling or greater boost to your soul than to live and die as a soldier! You will have all of eternity to enjoy a break from the battle.

KAI'RO: By the King's grace, I will stand. Everything you have said makes my heart burn inside me. I'm still pretty new to this whole thing. Pray for me.

ARMS DEALER: Well, it's time for you to go. I will pray fer ya. As with all good soldiers, I will see you on the other side of the River. Now go start fighting the good fight. It ends with your death.

CHAPTER NINE: DOIN' BATTLE

STORYTELLER: Kai'Ro left the Arms Dealer with his new armor. He appeared a little awkward in it at first, but the more he walked the more comfortable he looked. A few people stopped from time to time to watch him as he passed by on the path. Some pointed and sniggered, some looked confused, and a few others just stared. After a while Kai'Ro came into an open field. From the other side he saw a man approaching him in a nice dark suit. The man stopped Kai'Ro as they drew close. The suit he had on was very expensive. He had diamonds in his ears and a dark chain with a snake on it around his neck. There was a strange look in his eyes.

MAN: Where are you coming from?

KAI'RO: I'm from the City of Doom.

MAN: And where are you going?

KAI'RO: I'm on my way to the City of Gold.

MAN: So you're leaving the City of Doom? Why would you ever do that?

KAI'RO: Because that place is goin' to be judged by the King. It's an evil place full of evil people. I used to be a part of all that, but then I found out through the Preacher that if I stayed there that I was goin' to be judged along with the city.

MAN: Judged! That's crazy talk! For one, the City of Doom is a place of peace, pleasure, and prosperity. This road you're on now is a loaded with pain and loneliness. I bet the Preacher left that part out…

KAI'RO: Depends on what you mean by pain. Yeah, I know that life on this Heavenly Highway is hard and painful. But it isn't nearly as painful as the burden of my sinful conscience or the fear I had in my soul about dyin' without knowin' the King. When you talk about peace and pleasure in the City of Doom…it's not for real. I mean, that stuff is there for a while but it doesn't satisfy your soul. It's an awful and stinkin' place and I haven't had no regrets.

MAN: What is so awful about pleasure? Is it so wrong to get for yourself things that make you feel good? Things that make you powerful? It sounds like this King is keeping you from a lot of stuff that could make your life a whole lot better. What kind of King is *that*?

KAI'RO: That's one spin you can put on it, but like I said to you, that stuff just don't satisfy. It's like bein' real thirsty and tryin' to drink out of a cup with a bunch a holes in it. I mean, you can get a little in your mouth, but most of it just falls on the ground and leaves you thirsty. My whole life was like that cup for the longest. I kept puttin' stuff in it, but most of it just went right through me without satisfying my thirst. Besides that, most of the stuff that I was puttin' in my body and puttin' in my soul was poison. It was doin' some serious damage on me. Sex, drinkin', hustlin' and all that stuff is sheer poison, dawg. Sin is what it is, and it leads a brother to death. If you want to talk about pleasure, real pleasure is found in the King and in Him gettin' the glory. It's also found it walkin' His path of life. On that path He gives me joy and pleasures for real. His pleasures ain't necessarily money and fame, but they're peace, hope, and security. I've found pleasure and purpose on this road that I'm on now. That stuff back in the City of Doom wasn't no lastin' kind of pleasure.

MAN: So you left all of that in exchange for some promise of the King? What exactly is *He* giving to you that's so good? I can tell you right now that there's nothing down this road that will lead to happiness. This is a road of tears and frustration…

KAI'RO: Maybe, but who ever said that life's 'bout happiness anyway? What I got now is joy. I found joy at the Cross when my burden rolled away. I found out that I wasn't guilty no more and that I was no longer an enemy of the King. Happiness comes and goes. I used to be happy when I came home with a stack of dough from hustlin', but as soon as it was gone my happiness went wit it. It was the same with the girls and parties. The stuff just didn't stay. But joy, dawg…joy is buried deep down in my soul and no one can take that from me. I know that the King loves me and there's nothin' that can separate me from that love…no *man* can separate me, no *demons*, and not even *death* can separate me from the love the

King's got for me. That's pure *joy*, dawg.

STORYTELLER: As Kai'Ro continued to talk the Man fell back a little. Then to my surprise he started to change altogether. His skin grew shiny and scaly like the flesh of a snake. His suit started to rip apart as two large blacks wings burst from his back. Then he began to grow in size. Two red horns like the horns of a ram grew out of the side of his head, and fire and smoke emerged from his mouth. Long and sharp claws grew from his fingers like the talons of an eagle. He reared one of his hands back and took a swipe at Kai'Ro but just as he did so, Kai'Ro spun around and raised his Shield.

KAI'RO: How long did you think you could fool me with your smooth talk, Diablo? I know you're the prince of demons. You were tryin' to drag my heart back to my old ways, and you were tryin' to fill me with despair 'bout where I was goin'. I *recognized* your lies!

DIABLO: I have been waiting for you to come down this road and now you're all *mine!*

KAI'RO: I can tell you right now you best get outta my way or I'll send you home hoppin'.

DIABLO: Who are you to talk to me, you filthy human?

KAI'RO: I ain't no filthy human. I belong to the King of Kings and I am one of His sons. I'm made in the image of the King. I know who you are, you son of Hell, and I don't belong to you no more!

DIABLO: No, you are a son of my city, the City of Doom, and you belong to *me* you hopeless bastard. If you turn around to where you came from I will show you my mercy and spare your life.

KAI'RO: I can never go back! I'm in this thing for real. I'm no bastard. I was one once, but my Father is a King and He has purchased me from your stinkin' hands.

DIABLO: You have left the City of Doom, a place of pleasure and pride, for a life of hardship and pain. No good King would set you on such a path. If you stay on this path you are the stupidest man I have ever met! If you return, I will lavish upon you wealth, fame, and power. My ways were not harsh and my City was a place where you were great, O Kai'Ro of the City of Doom.

KAI'RO: That is no longer my name, you lyin' snake! I'm Kai'Ro the son of the King. I am a son of the City of Gold. It is true when you say that your ways were not harsh, and it is true that I was a great man in my old town. But I was under the Law, I was under wrath, and I was locked up in your doggone chains. You had plans to drag my soul wit you to Hell! Besides, all those things you promised me if I go back…they ain't yours anyway. Everything in this world belongs to the King…even you! Don't front like you got anything to offer me. You got nothin' to offer for real. In fact you're flat broke, dawg! You're just a puppet on strings. But either way I'm not goin' back. I will not give you my soul. The wealth and power that you're tryin' to pawn off on me is trash in comparison to what my King's got waitin' for me in His Kingdom. Now step off!

DIABLO: Where are you going to go, fool? Do you really think this King will accept you? *You,* a drug dealer, a man of violence, and a man who goes through women like a kid through a bag of candy? You have stolen from your own mother, cursed your neighbor, and lied to your pastor. You are an embarrassment. You have already failed multiple times on this journey of yours. Like an idiot, you fell into the Swamp of Despair. You lost your scroll just moments after you went to the loathsome Cross. At the Keeper's house you had lustful thoughts about his virgin daughters. You are a sick, sick impostor, Kai'Ro. Do you think this King of yours will allow someone as ugly and wretched as you into his house? Come back to *me* for you are like all of my children and I will let you do as you wish.

KAI'RO: All that you've said is true, but you forget that the King took all my stink and sin wit Him on the Cross. I'm clean as can be. He took all my sins and then He gave me His righteousness. You got *nothin'* on me! There is no condemnation for those who belong to the King. Back wit you I stood judged with every breath I took and I was on a speedin' highway to Hell. Naw! You best be goin' because I'll never place myself under you again. I will die before I go back to that life again.

DIABLO: Then you will get your wish, fool. I will thrash and throttle the very life out of you! Then, I'll drag your carcass back for your old friends to consider. They'll be rid of your foolish ideas forever.

KAI'RO: You're the fool, playa! You really don't get it do you? You kill me and then you send me to life for real. For me, to live in this life is to live for the King! But to die…man, to die is gain, dawg! You'll give me a one way ticket to the City of Gold and that's cool wit me. I can't wait to see my King face to face. Either way, you're goin' to be in for a brutal fight before you take this brotha down!

STORYTELLER: Diablo suddenly fired a hail of blazing darts at Kai'Ro. They came at him as thick as a cloud of angry hornets. Kai'Ro lifted up his Shield and the darts thudded against it like stones bouncing off of a tin roof. A few of them struck him in the foot, the shoulder, and the head. Kai'Ro stood his ground, but the fiery darts just kept coming and coming. He started to get tired. His Sword was pulled out, but Diablo stayed far enough away that he couldn't use it. More darts hit him and one snuck through and struck him right in the chest. He stumbled backwards. This battle lasted for hours as the prince demon fired dart after dart at him. I could see that the young warrior was getting more and more weary. For one second it looked like he was going to turn and run but then he saw the 116 on his shield and remembered what the Arms Dealer had told him. He stood his ground.

KAI'RO: (to himself) If I turn to run from this cat he'll light me up in the back and I'll fall for sure. Plus, if I resist the devil I'm sure he'll be the one that'll do the runnin' in the end.

STORYTELLER: I could tell that Diablo was getting frustrated with Kai'Ro's courage. He decided to make things more personal. He spread his wings apart and from behind his back he pulled out a flaming sword and a fiery ball and chain. On the hilt of the sword was the word SHAME and on the the ball and chain was the word DISCOURAGEMENT. These were powerful weapons. He charged at Kai'Ro hard and swung the ball and chain at him. The fiery ball crashed against Kai'Ro's shield like a blast of thunder. Kai'Ro's entire body shook. Then, the powerful demon came at him with his sword. Kai'Ro was able to knock back his first strike, but the second one got behind his Shield and gave him a huge wound in his side. Kai'Ro let out a yell and dropped his Sword. Diablo's red eyes flashed brightly and he swung his ball and chain one more time. Kai'Ro was able to get his Shield up a little this time, but the ball bounced off his Shield and almost knocked his Helmet off. Kai'Ro fell to the ground and gritted his teeth in pain. Almost all of the hope faded out of his eyes. Diablo stepped over him and grabbed him by his throat.

DIABLO: I told you that you belonged to *me*. You became mine the day you were born, you stupid fool. I gave you a chance to give up, turn around, and go back to business as usual. Now you're just damaged goods and I have no use for you any more. I'm going to spill your blood and snatch the life out of you.

STORYTELLER: Diablo raised his sword above him to deliver a final crushing blow. Yet as he did so, Kai'Ro reached out his arm as far as it would stretch and snatched his Sword that had fallen on the ground. He drove the blade deep into Diablo's stomach and screamed a great shout of victory!

KAI'RO: Rejoice not over me, O my enemy; when I fall; I shall rise…

STORYTELLER: Diablo groaned in pain and a long trail of bright red fire burst from his mouth and his eyes. He spread his great wings and took off into the air cursing and howling until he disappeared over some hills. Kai'Ro gasped and let out a breath of relief. He rolled over onto his bloodied hands and knees. He was badly hurt and could barely stand up. Limping over to a rock, he sat down to rest for a moment.

KAI'RO: (in prayer) Thank you, Father, for savin' my life from the devil. I rejoice that You who are in me is greater than he who is in the world. Please give me the strength to keep goin'. I'm hurt bad.

STORYTELLER: Kai'Ro pulled out his old Bible and read some words of encouragement. As he read he felt a bit stronger. He drank some water and ate some food that the Keeper had given him. Then he returned to his reading and read, "Let us then with confidence draw near to the throne of grace, that we may receive mercy and find grace to help in time of need."

Kai'Ro smiled and closed his eyes.

CHAPTER TEN: THE ALLEY OF THE SHADOW OF DEATH

STORYTELLER: Kai'Ro was able to get himself together and he started down the Heavenly Highway again. His armor had taken a real beating, but it had saved his life. He walked on for a while down the Highway until it appeared to dip down into a long dark Alley. He stopped for a moment to look. The Alley was full of a thick smog and I could hear strange and evil noises rumbling from the deep. Kai'Ro swallowed hard and just then a man came running towards him from out of the Alley. He had on armor like Kai'Ro but he was missing his Sword and his helmet was about to fall off.

KAI'RO: Yo, man, where you goin'?

DESERTER: Man, don't even think about goin' down there, dawg! I barely made it out of there with my life. That place is as scary as hell! I ain't lyin'.

KAI'RO: Yeah, you ain't lyin'. It looks real scary to me too. That doesn't mean I'm not gonna go down there.

DESERTER: There were things down there that I've never seen before, homie. I mean, there was some crazy monsters, goblins, ghosts, all kinds 'a stuff. There's a Cloud of Confusion and you can't see nothin'. The whole place is full of Death. I split outta there so fast. There was no way I was gonna try to make it through there.

KAI'RO: Maybe if we go together we can keep each other safe. Two is better than one, right?

DESERTER: Naw, dawg. This is as far as I'm gonna go.

KAI'RO: There's no goin' back for a true soldier of the King. You should know that! Get yourself together, man, 'cause you can't go back now.

DESERTER: Man, bump this! I told you I ain't goin' down there again. If you got any brains you won't do it either, homie.

STORYTELLER: Kai'Ro frowned as Deserter ran off. He turned to face the dark Alley before him. He tightened the chin strap on his helmet, pulled out his Sword and started walking. As he descended into the mouth of the Alley it grew darker and darker. Before long the sun itself appeared to vanish until there was hardly any light at all. The air was hot and thick with smoke and strange shadows seemed to race back and forth across the main road. He found himself walking a long stretch of cracked-concrete. At first things were strangely quiet like a town from a zombie movie. On either side of the road were thick grey brick walls that rose up so high that no one could climb them. In certain parts of the walls were large holes and cracks. If anyone was to make it through this Alley they would have to go straight through it. Up ahead was a metal garbage can with burning trash inside. Two cloaked creatures glared at Kai'Ro as he drew near. Strange orange eyes burned inside the cloaks and they had sharp, taloned fingers like bird claws. They slashed them at him and hissed. Kai'Ro held up his Sword at them and they slunk back. Occasionally a street lamp would flicker on and off. At one point, one of the lights flashed and I saw a faded green street sign which read BAD MEMORIES BOULEVARD. The road narrowed quite a bit as Kai'Ro continued to walk. Some strange red lights along the walls were the only things that gave Kai'Ro an idea where to go. Up ahead I saw a young man in a black T-shirt mercilessly kicking and beating another young man who was rolling around on the ground and begging for help. Kai'Ro saw that the man on the ground didn't have much left. He ran up to help.

KAI'RO: Hey, dawg, what'cha doin? Lay off! You hear me? Lay off that dude!

STORYTELLER: Kai'Ro raced up to the young man who was laying out the beating and put his hand on his shoulder to stop him. The young man in the black T-shirt spun around. Kai'Ro jumped back in shock. The face staring back at him was his own. The other Kai'Ro burst into laughter and took off running into the shadows. When Kai'Ro was able to regain his senses he stooped down to help the young man on the ground. The guy was bleeding badly out of his nose, his mouth, and his ears.

KAI'RO: Hey, man, it's alright now. He's gone. You're gonna be alright.

STORYTELLER: The man on the ground started hollering at Kai'Ro and trying to squirm out of his grasp.

MAN: Naw, get away from me! Why won't you leave me alone? What'd I ever do to you?

STORYTELLER: Kai'Ro looked down at the man and tried to help him again. Then, the man just disappeared like a puff of smoke.

KAI'RO: (sadly) I remember that poor dude. I put that cat in the hospital for like two weeks all because I thought he was the one talkin' to my girl. Man, I messed that guy up for nothin'. Can't believe I did that…

STORYTELLER: Unsure of what to do, Kai'Ro decided to keep going. He was bothered. He went on a ways further until he spotted a young man in a bright red shirt rummaging hurriedly through a big black purse. The young man looked up every now and then as if he was listening for someone. Just beyond this young man I spotted a little boy in the shadows watching the other man going through the purse. Kai'Ro came up closer to the thief, but as soon as he got within a few feet the other young man turned to face him. Just like earlier, the face of the one staring back at him was his own. The young thief smiled a big smile at Kai'Ro, burst into laughter and then took off running. As he did so Kai'Ro saw the little boy in the shadows and a look of total embarrassment covered his face.

KAI'RO: Ah, naw…*not* my 'lil brotha. Come here, Lil' One! Come here. Your big bro ain't like that no more. I don't steal from moms no more. C'mon, Lil' One. Don't run off, shortie! Come back here!

STORYTELLER: Lil' One just burst into tears, shook his head at Kai'Ro and then ran off deep into the shadows. But then, just down the way, another Kai'Ro look-alike was leaning on the wall smoking a joint. Just beyond him was his brother, Lil' One, watching through a window in one of the walls. Then another Kai'Ro appeared with a backpack on. He was walking with two friends and talking.

KAI'RO LOOK-ALIKE: This is the last day I'm goin' to school, dawg. How much have we learned in the last two years? Man, we ain't learned nothin'! I was talkin' to Dealer just yesterday and he said he could hook all of us up if we wanted to start hustlin'. I told him I was down, what about ya'll?

STORYTELLER: I watched this Kai'Ro take his backpack full of school books and sling it into a dumpster. The two boys that were with him did the same thing. Just like before, Lil' One was walking a few feet behind them the whole time listening. He stopped at the dumpster, looked at it for a minute, and then stared after his brother as he walked off into the distance. Lil' One took his own backpack off, tossed it into the dumpster, and then walked off in a different direction. At this point the real Kai'Ro folded both of his hands over his face and started to cry.

KAI'RO: O God, don't let this be for real! I'm so sorry 'bout all that stuff. I pray that my little brotha didn't see me do all that terrible stuff. Don't let Lil' One go down the same road as me, *please*. I'm beggin' you, God! Please don't let him make the same mistakes as me. Please! I'm cryin' out to you to restore the locust years to my little brotha. Please make right whatever I made wrong by my own mistakes. Only you can fix this for real. I messed up so bad, but I know you can make anything right again if you're willin'.

STORYTELLER: There were more Kai'Ro look-alikes going on for almost as far as the eye could see. They were fighting, cursing, stealing, and wandering around with scandalous looking girls. Kai'Ro started to turn around but as he did so a small glimmer of light flashed on the outside of his shield showing him the 116. He let out a deep sigh and looked up toward heaven even though there was no way he could see it right from the alley.

KAI'RO: (to himself) If anyone is the King's son, he is a new creation. The old has passed away; behold the new has come. Thank you, my King. I don't have to live in my past as ugly as it is. I can forget what's behind me and press on towards what's before me. By your grace I'll go on…

STORYTELLER: As Kai'Ro prayed, the alley cleared and he was able to walk for a while without any more bad memories appearing before him. Then BAD MEMORIES BOULEVARD ended. Within a short distance he came to STRANGLE-HOPE STREET. This street was narrow and even darker than the boulevard he had just left. There were horrible noises bouncing off the walls and coming towards Kai'Ro. There were groans, shrieks, and loud roars. Kai'Ro swallowed hard and hesitated for the moment. He pulled his Shield close to his body and raised his Sword.

KAI'RO: (to himself) If the King is for me…who can be against me?

STORYTELLER: He plunged into the street. The further he went, the narrower the street became. It wasn't long before he almost had to turn sideways just to fit. The metal of his Shield and Breastplate actually scraped up against the walls and he was forced to move slowly. Just then, a slimy arm from out of a hole in the wall grabbed him around the throat. Kai'Ro yelled and struggled until he was able to free himself. He hadn't gone far before something white and ugly like a ghost came down upon him and tried to push him through a hole in the wall. Kai'Ro flailed at the spirit with his Sword until it released him. Behind the walls there was a horrible roaring sound and loud thuds as if a huge creature on the other side was trying to break through the walls and devour him . Sometimes sudden explosions of fire would shoot out from the walls and blast against Kai'Ro's Shield pinning him against the wall behind him. This terrible Street went on for miles and Kai'Ro was only able to go at a slow pace because there was hardly any room to move. I saw a skinny spirit sneak up behind him. The spirit was shriveled and decayed like a corpse. It came up close to Kai'Ro until it's disgusting face was right on his shoulder. It started to whisper spiteful things into his ears. It whispered horrible things about the King and about His Kingdom. For a moment it was obvious that Kai'Ro was ashamed because he believed that these thoughts were his own. Then he cried out:

KAI'RO: I gotta take every thought captive. Naw! Get off me, you foul demon. Get ya poison outta my head! Those thoughts ain't my thoughts. That's poison from Hell!

STORYTELLER: The ugly spirit disappeared into the darkness, but instantly three little red goblins scurried down the walls and climbed on top of Kai'Ro. One of them had a little hammer with the word IRRITATION on it and he started beating him in the face and on the head with the hammer. Kai'Ro tried to knock it off, but the goblin was too quick and would dodge his blows and then smack him again from a different angle. One of the other goblins snuck down on his legs and started sticking him with a sharp pin called WEARINESS. The more he stuck him the slower Kai'Ro moved. He swatted at this goblin, but like the first one he was too quick and avoided all of Kai'Ro's blows. The third goblin had a syringe full of a liquid called FEAR. He jabbed it into Kai'Ro's neck just below his Helmet. At this point Kai'Ro stumbled to his knees and His Sword fell from his limp hands.

KAI'RO: I can't go no further in this evil place…

STORYTELLER: With what strength he had left he picked up his Sword and struggled to his feet. With a lot of effort he was able to turn his body around. The goblins started laughing and hitting and sticking him even more. But just then a voice came echoing down the alley walls. It was the voice of another man, and the man was reciting the 23rd Psalm, "…Tho I walk thru the Alley of the Shadow of Death, I will fear no evil. For you are with me. Your rod and your staff, they comfort me…"

Kai'Ro spun back the other way again with a look of joy on his face and he hollered out.

KAI'RO: Hey dawg, don't leave me. Lemme catch up to you! Wait up!

STORYTELLER: His voice bounced off a ways down the walls, but there was no response. Still Kai'Ro was encouraged and started moving forward again with more speed and determination than he had before. The goblins continued hitting and sticking him, but he didn't appear to notice anymore. After a while they snarled, gave up and scurried back up the walls again like rats up a drainpipe. There were still slimy and scaly arms that grabbed at Kai'Ro through the walls. At one point he could hardly move because there were so many arms and hands grasping, pushing and pulling at him. Some tried to peel off his Helmet and others struggled to rip his Shield out of his hands. Kai'Ro slashed and lashed with his Sword and tried to beat them back so that he could continue going. He gritted his teeth.

KAI'RO: I will fear no evil in this Alley. Even here…the King is with me…there's nowhere for me to go where He ain't already there watchin' me. I gotta press on. I gotta keep goin'!

STORYTELLER: The strange creatures in the walls grew more aggressive. A few actually crawled out of their holes like worms out of the ground. They had razor-edged teeth and pointed red eyes. They hissed and spat and tried to slash at Kai'Ro with their claws or sink their fangs into his flesh. His Sword and Shield were excellent weapons in this place and he was able to beat most of his attackers back into their holes. Yet every now and then he would get scratched or bitten and he would yell out in pain. Then suddenly he shook free from all the aggressive monsters like one falling through a wall of thick branches. He fell into an open space again where he was able to stand and move about with more freedom. When he stood up, there before him was something that nearly caused him to fall out. It was a large black hole with a narrow cement bridge running across the middle of it. The bridge itself had a slick green moss growing on top of it. Just before the bridge was an old crumbled sign with graffiti on it that read: "The blind lead the blind." Kai'Ro eased up to the edge of the Pit and looked down. It was full of bones and bodies. There was a foul smell coming up from out of it. It was dark, but I could see that some of the bodies were still moving a little and they were groaning and crying for help but they were far too deep in the Pit for any person to pull them out.

KAI'RO: Man, I don't know about this. It reminds me of that Pit that David fell into a long time ago. I've come so far through this horrible place, but that bridge is so doggone slick, and if I fall off one way or the other I'm really done for. I wanna go back, but maybe I'm almost outta here.

STORYTELLER: As Kai'Ro waited at the edge of the bridge thinking, I saw another man already walking a ways down from where

Kai'Ro was standing. Kai'Ro looked up and spotted him too. The other man was walking quickly but carefully so that he wouldn't slip.

KAI'RO: If that cat can make it, then so can I. That's gotta be that same dude from earlier. Maybe if I can catch up to him we can hang out and do this whole thing together.

STORYTELLER: So Kai'Ro stepped out onto the bridge. It was slipperier than he thought and he almost lost his footing and fell into the Pit after his first step. As he was flailing his arms and trying to regain his balance he looked down into the Pit and he saw a decaying body covered and surrounded by a bunch of CDs that Kai'Ro used to listen to.

KAI'RO: Man, I remember listenin' to all that stuff…those CDs were like my Bible back then. What those guys said to me was the truth. Those rappers *were* the truth to me back then…hip-hop used to be my father…but now the King is my daddy.

STORYTELLER: He regained his balance and started walking again. He was more careful with each step this time but the bridge itself started to zig-zag back and forth and everything around him grew darker and darker until he couldn't even see the next step in front of him. He was forced to stop because he knew that his next step could be his last.

KAI'RO: What do I do now? It's so dark that I can't go forward or backwards 'cause I'll fall for sure.

STORYTELLER: Kai'Ro stood there hopelessly for a minute and like anyone who is lost and confused, he started to panic. But then a small light appeared around him. It was just a faint glow, but it caught his eyes and he looked down.

KAI'RO: Aw, c'mon, Kai'Ro, you're such a fool! You got a way outta this mess right wit you now.

STORYTELLER: Kai'Ro reached into his back pocket and pulled out his Bible. As he opened it a shaft of light shot out and gave him just enough light to see the next step in front of him. Kai'Ro's entire face lit up with joy and he began to speak words from his Bible.

KAI'RO: Your Word is lamp unto my feet and a light unto my path! No wonder so many folks have fallen off this road…without this Word they're walkin' this dark road in total blindness!

STORYTELLER: He kept his Word open for the remainder of the bridge. The road remained slick, and even though he was still frightened by the horrible stuff in the Pit below he was able to make it to the other side. Just as he crossed over, a thin beam of sunlight started to push through the darkness and the fog. I could see that the Alley actually started to ascend up onto level ground again. Kai'Ro started to move quickly, anxious to leave the horrible Alley behind him. The further he climbed out the brighter it became. At one point he stopped and looked behind him. From this high point he could see most of the Alley laid bare. He saw the thin bridge crossing the Pit and he saw the terrible STRANGLE-HOPE STREET with all the monsters and goblins. As the light pushed further onto the Alley all of the evil things shrieked and ducked into the holes in the walls. It was a holy light that shone down on the Alley and all the evil below gave way to it. Kai'Ro turned around again with a big smile on his face. Just up ahead was another man like him. He had on the same armor covering some baggy jeans and a white-T. From this distance Kai'Ro recognized the man and he yelled to him.

KAI'RO: Phanatik! It's me, Kai'Ro, dawg! Wait up!

CHAPTER ELEVEN:
CATCHIN' UP

STORYTELLER: Phanatik pressed on, refusing to turn around. It was obvious that he was in a hurry to get out of the Alley too. Kai'Ro decided to sprint to catch up. Before long he closed in on Phanatik. Starting to feel good about his progress, he raced right by him and went on until he suddenly tripped and fell down hard. He laid there for a while until Phanatik caught up to him and helped him to his feet.

KAI'RO: Thanks, homie.

STORYTELLER: Kai'Ro felt embarrassed as Phanatik pulled him to his feet.

KAI'RO: Man, Phanatik! I can't believe it's really you, dawg.

PHANATIK: Yeah, frat. I heard you headed off down this Highway.

KAI'RO: I had no idea you were on this road too, man. Then, the Keeper told me that you had passed through.

PHANATIK: Yeah, when I heard you had left the City of Doom and that you took off on this trip, I was like 'Man, I gotta catch up and we can do this thing together.' You left just before I could catch up with you.

STORYTELLER: The two of them started walking side by side down the road and decided to talk about their journeys so far .

KAI'RO: Man, I had no idea you were feelin' this whole thing. I had no clue that you were thinkin' about comin' along.

PHANATIK: Yeah, the Preacher caught up with me 'bout the same time he got with you. I had been goin' through some stuff in my life around that time and was really lookin' for hope. Before I met him I was givin' my all to the thug life, ya know? I mean, I was into the hustlin' real deep and I was makin' more money than a man knows what to do with. You knew what I was up to and you saw how I was livin'.

KAI'RO: Yeah, you were livin' large. Everybody knew your name.

PHANATIK: It just wasn't sittin' right with me. I had everything goin' for me, but inside I was just feelin' terrible. It wasn't really that long before I ran into Preacher. I was chillin' one day in one of my Benzs and he just rolled up on me. I thought he was trippin' and I even reached for my piece the way he came up on me, but when he opened his mouth and started talkin' to me about my life and how miserable I was, I just couldn't do nothin' but listen to what he was sayin'. Somehow he just knew about all the drama that was goin' on inside my head. But then when he started talkin' 'bout this Heavenly Highway and that there was a way to get right with God, I was like 'Man, what this cat is sayin' is dope for real.' He told me I'd have to put the hustlin' aside forever if I was goin' to do this thing. When he said that, I started feelin' this burden on my back, but I was I thinkin' there was no way I could do that. I mean, how could I give up the lifestyle I had goin' with the girls, the cash, and the pleasure. But I felt all torn up inside. I guess it's when I heard that you had taken off on the same journey that I decided I could prob'ly do it too. I mean, you and I were never really friends for real, but you were the guy who had my respect...

KAI'RO: That's tight, dawg. My story is pretty much the same.

STORYTELLER: Kai'Ro told Phanatik about the first stage of his journey when he and Quitter and Follower stopped off at the House of Mockers. He mentioned how they fell into the Swamp of Discouragement and then how Quitter and Follower left him high and dry.

PHANATIK: Yeah, those two cats came runnin' back to the City of Doom like two scared puppies. They was all covered in mud and stuff and it was like they was tryin' to duck and dodge back to their houses. But everybody knew they had gone wit you, and when they came back they tried so hard to play the whole thing off. Nobody was buyin' it though. Everyone started crackin' on those guys so bad for how they punked out like that. Man, it wouldn't let up. Those two fools were so humiliated that they hardly came out of the house no more. It would a been better for them if they had drowned in that Swamp because they came back lookin' like a bunch of scared clowns.

KAI'RO: Yeah, it's like they just dropped out of the race. It's better to never start racin' or fightin' if you ain't gonna finish what you started. So I 'spose you ran into Worldly Wiseman?

PHANATIK: Naw. I never saw that dude. After hearin' all about your little adventure in the Swamp I was able to find the foot path and keep myself from fallin' in. After I got down the path a ways it started to get dark. I was lookin' for a place to crash and that's when I ran into a beautiful girl named Bliss. This girl was too fine. She had a little house just 'round the way and when I was goin' by, she was standin' there in the door like she was watchin' for me or somethin'. She had on these 'lil shorts and a tight shirt that was leavin' nothin' up to the imagination. That girl had one of those looks on her face that can a draw a brotha in. She called out to me as I was walkin' by. She said, "Hey, boy, come here. My man has gone off to town for business and he won't be back for 'bout two weeks. I've covered my bed with silk sheets and filled my room with some of the sweetest perfume a girl can buy. I've been to church and said my prayers, and now I'm ready for a little enjoyment. Why don't you come in here and spend some time with a lonely girl? I won't disappoint you." Dawg, I was tempted about as much as a brotha can be tempted.

KAI'RO: I hope you kept going, 'cause that girl's house leads to death!

PHANATIK: Yeah, I know dude, but it took me and my thick head a minute or two to figure it out. I made a bad mistake. I got off the path and took a step towards her house, and when I got up by her door, man, that girl grabbed me and kissed me like I've never been kissed before.

KAI'RO: What were you thinkin', dawg?

PHANATIK: That's the thing…I *wasn't* thinkin'. At least I wasn't thinkin' with my heart. She pulled me into the bedroom and just like she said there were silk sheets and the room smelled better than anything I'd smelled before. She had some candles burnin'. We were 'bout to do our thing when I saw the blood.

KAI'RO: The blood?

PHANATIK: Yeah. There was a bunch a sticky blood pooled up under the bed. It was a lot a blood, homie. I took one look at that blood, looked back at her, and then I dipped about as fast as a brotha' can run. She snatched at me and screamed at me to come back, but I was gone, dude.

KAI'RO: Man, girls like Bliss are a slaughter house. You was like a lamb led to the slaughter. Girls like that can ruin a man for real. How many guys do you and I know who've seen their lives end in a place like hers?

PHANATIK: Too many.

KAI'RO: You remember Lustful? He couldn't get enough girls. That poor fool got AIDs and died like two years ago. What about that cat named Playa? Man, that boy's got like three or four kids to support and he can't even hardly hold down a job. Girls like Bliss? Shoot, there's a thousand ways they can kill a brotha.

PHANATIK: I know, frat. You tellin' the truth. It was the King's grace that got me outta there. Girls like Bliss have been a weakness for me as long as I can remember. I found out early on that just 'cause you start off on this Highway those temptations don't go away. It's been the King's good grace to me that after all those girls I been with in the past that I never got no disease and never got no girl pregnant. I mean that ain't just bein' lucky, dawg. That's just the King protectin' me from disaster. With Bliss it was like the King gave me new eyes…take me back a few months and there's no way I see the blood and the fact that she was a killa. I would of been in some trouble for real! Who knows what woulda happened to me?

KAI'RO: I'm glad you came to your senses, homie. When I ran into Worldly Wiseman I almost made a bad decision too. He told me I could lose my burden headin' up to Legalopolis and gettin' a cat named Mac-Morality to remove the thing for me. I made a bad mistake and listened to him. Fortunately for me the Preacher caught up with me and set me straight.

PHANATIK: Yeah, praise the King, for the Preacher. The man found me just a short while after I ran from Bliss's house. He warned me that my flesh was still very much alive and that things might even get tougher the closer I got to the Cross. I appreciated him because he was there for me. He could tell that I was real down, and he kinda jumped on me for bein' so stupid, but at the same time he encouraged me and prayed for me. That did a lot to keep me goin'.

STORYTELLER: The two continued to talk. They both shared stories about some of the different travelers that they ran into on the way. They both had similar experiences in Birdville and Rock City. Like Kai'Ro, Phanatik steered clear of Thornville, even though he said it was a strong temptation for him to check it out.

KAI'RO: What'd you think when the Arms Dealer first handed you that armor?

PHANATIK: I ain't gonna lie. I didn't like it much at first 'cause it felt goofy and I knew it was goin' to stand out. I was already feelin' the pressure of just givin' my life to the King and promisin' to follow after Him, but the armor made it clear that if I was in this thing for real, I was really going to stand out.

KAI'RO: Yeah, but it came in useful against that devil, Diablo, didn't it?

PHANATIK: Naw, I never saw him.

KAI'RO: That prince-demon 'bout killed me! This armor and the Sword saved my life.

PHANATIK: Well, I had to tussle with a few of the monsters in that awful Alley back there.

KAI'RO: That was a scary place, dawg.

PHANATIK: Scary as Hell! It kinda came out of nowhere. I remember dippin' down a ways in the path and it was like I was just wanderin' through a ghost town or somethin,' but then the sun went down. As soon as the sun was gone it was like somebody opened the gates of Hell. I mean I had monsters comin' out of God knows where. These things were huge and scary and a few of them woulda' killed me if it hadn't been for this armor and Sword. I almost turned back at a few points because I couldn't see any hope in sight...

KAI'RO: Me neither. It was like hope got snuffed out down there. I felt like David when he said he found himself in that miry pit. I hope that place is behind us *forever.*

PHANATIK: Yeah, me too. But the Preacher said that there would be lots of different Alleys in this journey that would be dark places where our faith and hope would be put to the test. I hope that that awful Alley back there was the worst of them.

KAI'RO: Maybe that experience will make us stronger next time so that we won't be so quick to feel like runnin'.

STORYTELLER: In my dream I saw how much this time with Phanatik benefitted Kai'Ro. To find a friend who made the same powerful choice and was willing to walk it out was a huge encouragement to him. They talked and talked for a long time about what they both saw at the Interpreter's house and other adventures from the trip. Then the subject turned to the Cross.

KAI'RO: You gotta tell me about how you felt when you got to the Cross, dawg!

PHANATIK: Aw, man, how do you describe *those* kinds of feelin's? I mean I felt a bunch of things. I felt like the whole script of my life got flipped for real. I felt things comin' and felt things goin'. Like I felt accepted for real. I felt like I had a big Dad and that made me feel like I had a family. I never really had a pops 'cause my old man ran out on me right after I was born. But when I felt His grace and acceptance comin' on me I felt so alive, dawg, just so alive!

KAI'RO: And what'd you feel goin'?

PHANATIK: Shame. Guilt. Embarrassment. Fear of judgment. All that stuff just rolled down the hill into that open grave with my burden. It was like all the baggage I had been carryin' around in my soul just disappeared. I felt clean all over for the very first time in my life. What went tumblin' down that hill, man, was a bunch of terrible things. I mean a bunch of terrible things I had done, frat. When the stain and guilt for all those things was washed away I felt as free as a bird.

KAI'RO: You ain't lyin', homie. My rap sheet was over a mile long too. It felt unbelievable to know that the King took the blame for a guy like me. When the Preacher first showed me how all my sins offended God and that I was eternally separated from Him because of my sin I almost lost hope. I mean when he told me that the debt of my sins meant that I had to spend eternity in Hell I felt about as bad a brotha can feel. But then when he told me that the King had paid my sin-debt on that Cross I couldn't believe it. I mean my sins were just too ugly...that was unbelievable love that He just stepped into my shoes and took the blame for me so that God and I could be in right relationship again. I mean who'd *do* somethin' like that? There's a few cats that might take a bullet for a friend, but it's like He took a fatal bullet for the whole world....even for folks that don't know Him or even hate Him.

PHANATIK: Yeah, and to think that He was perfect. I mean, He never did anything wrong...not even once and yet He was willin' to die for a dude as ugly as me just so that I could have a right relationship with God again...it's amazin', dawg! Simply amazin'.

CHAPTER TWELVE:
REVEREND RELEVANT
PASTOR & PATHETIC

STORYTELLER: As the two continued to talk about the amazing

STORYTELLER: As the two continued to talk about the amazing sacrifice of the King on the Cross I saw in my dream a gigantic church. It was made of bright red bricks and the steeple seemed to almost touch the clouds. There were large stained glass windows and the grounds around the church were covered in beautiful flowers and bushes. There were two men standing on the bright white steps leading up to the church entrance and they were having a tense conversation. One of the men, the pastor of the church, was a middle-aged man dressed in an expensive dark suit. He had a white silken kerchief sticking out of the pocket on his suit coat. There were shiny black shoes on his feet. The other man was dressed in an older brown suit that was rather plain. His shoes were a little shabby and he was carrying a small plastic bag full of canned goods. I perceived that the flashy dressed man was named Pastor Pathetic and the man in the brown suit was Reverend Relevant. Kai'Ro and Phanatik came upon their conversation along the Highway.

PASTOR PATHETIC: Listen, I hear what you're saying. There's a lot of people in Struggle-Town that need food, shelter, and help. Those of us at Me-Myself-and-I Chapel would really love to help you guys down at In-His-Service but right now we can't do a whole lot.

REV. RELEVANT: I just don't get it, brother. How can you turn your back on all those people? I mean, who's going to tell these people about the King? Who's going to show them that the King is a good King if it isn't our two churches?

PASTOR PATHETIC: Look, you know about our new church. A lot of the folks in my church got tired of worshipping in Struggle-Town. You know, it's dirty there. The crime has gone up a lot the past few years, and most of the people at the church stopped feeling safe down there. So I got with my deacons and some of the leaders and we decided we'd start worshipping out where everybody felt better. So, that's why we've got a multi-million dollar place right here on the edge of Happyville. Happyville's a nice town, brother. So with all of our money tied up in our new church right now, I can't go to my people and ask them to support your soup kitchen or whatever it was you mentioned…

REV. RELEVANT: It's the School for the Lost Sheep…a school for fatherless boys and girls. It saddens me to see you guys just up and leave Struggle-Town like that. You and I grew up there. Your church was a real cornerstone in that community going all the way back to when your great-grandfather founded it. Now your old church is just a big empty building…it's like another symbol of abandonment for the people there. It seems like so many churches are just tucking and running these days.

PASTOR PATHETIC: What do you mean tucking and running? Is it a bad thing to get my people out of a no-good neighborhood and bring them some place safe where they don't have to worry about their cars gettin' busted into during the service? We're focused on taking our kids out of that garbage dump and giving them a real chance. We have the Keep Our Kids Clean Multi-Purpose Center with three full-sized basketball courts. We have a skating rink and our Crunk for the King Teen Sanctuary where they can have some amazing concerts and youth rallies. We got places now where our youth can stay out of trouble. You gotta start thinking about the kids at some point, brother.

REV. RELEVANT: Yeah, but what about all the kids left walking the streets? Not every kid and every family has the means to get up and out of the hood like most of the families at your church. What about the kids looking for role models? There's kids looking for good things to get involved with in the afternoon. Not everyone is gang banging and not everyone is into the drug scene. That's why I was asking you to consider helping with our School for the Lost Sheep where we can offer some of the poor kids in Struggle-Town a real education, an introduction to the King and to His plans for them. Our school is already giving kids an alternative to the gangs and street life. We're trying to give the youth in that area some kind of community and family outside the streets. Diablo is peddling a lot of stuff to the people in Struggle-Town because there aren't too many alternatives. But he isn't offering any hope…he's offering violence, pain, and addiction. We want our church to bring the King's hands and feet to the streets of Struggle-Town by offering them real hope. That's why we put our bodies there, and that's why In-His-Service isn't leaving. I'm just afraid that by moving out to Happyville, you and your church aren't going to be making much of an impact anymore.

STORYTELLER: Pastor Pathetic started to frown. I could see that he was about to lose his temper.

PASTOR PATHETIC: Impact! I've got almost four thousand people that come to hear me preach every Sunday. Through satellite almost another six thousand people tune in to hear what I got to say. Our mass choir has sung all over the world. They've recorded three platinum selling CDs. I have two best-selling books, *The Blessings of the King* and *O the Ways the King Seeks to Bless You My Child*. My congregation brings in almost ten million dollars each year in tithe. Don't talk to me about impact, brother. Me-Myself-and-I is making an impact!

STORYTELLER: Kai'Ro and Phanatik had been listening quietly the whole time. Kai'Ro started getting a little irritated and he stepped into the conversation.

KAI'RO: Excuse me. I know I'm kinda butting in on this conversation, but this whole debate has got my attention. You said that your church tithes almost ten million dollars a year. I mean that's phenomenal. About how much of that money makes it out to bless other people?

PASTOR PATHETIC: (laughing nervously) That's tough to say, son. Like I said to my brother here earlier, almost everything right now is going to the bank to pay for our church. We've got roller skating rinks, basketball courts, and a church that can seat five thousand people. That's not cheap!

KAI'RO: With all due respect, it seems like Me-Myself-and-I is mainly concerned with *itself*. I mean, it seems from what I've read in the word that the King wanted the Church to be a tool for bringin' His Kingdom to a sin-strangled world. As I've read it, the King's people are supposed to bring hope to the hopeless, food to the hungry, clothing to the naked, and love to the hated. From everything I've heard you say, it sounds like you guys are doin' none of those things. In fact, I'd even say that your church is more worried about its own needs and good times that it doesn't even notice the needs just down the road.

PASTOR PATHETIC: Maybe you're hard of hearing, son. Did you not hear me say that I have over four thousand people in my church and over six thousand that tune in on the television? Most of those people were hopeless and hungry at one time. Now I've got almost ten thousand people that have found hope and happiness. Do the math. My brother, Reverend Relevant has a church of what…two hundred and fifty? Who do you think the King is going to be happier with…ten thousand or two hundred and fifty?

KAI'RO: You're right. You've got a lot more people sitting in your pews. But from the sounds of things that's all any of those people are ever going to do. *Sit.* I mean my brother, Reverend Relevant, is trying to make disciples. From everything I've heard he's tryin' to equip His people to get out on the streets and bring the King to the people through acts of service and ministry. They aren't wastin' their lives. Be honest. How's a skatin' rink going to make disciples? Yeah, it'll give your people's kids something to do on a Saturday night…maybe keep them out of trouble…but not much more than that. Beyond all that, it sounds like you pulled up roots on the very community your great-granddaddy tried to help. I thought the church was 'sposed to be salt and light. You know…it was called to help keep a community stable and to keep shooing away the darkness by tellin' people about the Gospel and *showing* them the Gospel. Seems like you and your church just snuffed your light right out. If you aren't meeting the needs in the street and in the world around you then you're just another building.

STORYTELLER: For a minute Pastor Pathetic was stunned silent. He stared hard at Kai'Ro as if he were thinking carefully about what he was going to say next.

PASTOR PATHETIC: The King came to this earth, son, to make people happy. Without Him the whole world is a real sad place. My mission and the mission of my church is to make people happy in the King. We want people to hear how much the King loves them and how much He wants to make their life better. There are thousands and thousands of people at my church who have heard that message and they've found that happiness. Our lives are happy. Our church is a happy place.

REV. RELEVANT: But that's just it, brother. Didn't the King say that the harvest was plentiful but that the workers were few? I agree that the King wants us to know that He loves us and wants to make our lives better, but then He wants us to take that message to anyone who hasn't heard or experienced that message yet. We're hardwired to go after what makes us happy and if we aren't care-ful we can keep that happy message and that happy focus all to ourselves while the rest of the world is being strangled by misery, addiction, and hopelessness. I think that the King wants us to find our joy in two things. One, He wants us to find our joy in Him. He wants us to discover that only a relationship with Him is what matters. Two, He wants us to find our joy in working with Him to bring a message of hope to a dying world. Seems like Me-Myself-and-I have found their joy in their own happiness, and until you understand part two, I have to agree with this young man here... your church is just going to become another nice building on the other side of town. I wish you would reconsider what I've asked you today. It would be a benefit to Struggle-Town for your people to give generously to some of the programs that I've mentioned. In fact, they could even volunteer at some of those programs. It would also benefit your people because they'd experience joy like never before once they start joining the King in the work He's try-ing to do in our town.

PASTOR PATHETIC: I hear you, but like I said, our money is tied up in a huge mortgage note, and keeping our many programs go-ing. We can't help you. And honestly, my people aren't *interested* in helping with that stuff anyway. It's time for me to be going. I have a sermon I need to prepare.

REV. RELEVANT: The greatest sermon you could ever preach is for your people to see you walking the streets of Struggle-Town again...bringing hope and life to your old community.

STORYTELLER: Pastor Pathetic gave Kai'Ro, Phanatik, and Rev-erend Relevant a passing wave and walked off quickly down the path.

KAI'RO: Sorry to crash your conversation like that. I just couldn't help but say somethin'.

REV. RELEVANT: (sighing) It's tough, son. It's getting harder and harder to get churches anywhere to step foot into gritty places. Some of them will cut a check from time to time, but to actually get laborers in this harvest down here…well…it's almost impossible.

KAI'RO: Well, I think churches like Me-Myself-And-I have lost their voice in the world. In fact, I think they're givin' the King a bad name. People see all the drama and pain in the world and they see a lot of so-called followers of the King just locked away in their praise palaces down the road. It's like they don't even notice or care about all the hurt that's goin' on all around them. The King lived a life of carin' and givin' and then when those who claim they're following Him don't do the same…man…it's just embarrassing.

STORYTELLER: Reverend Relevant held up the small sack of groceries in his hands.

REV. RELEVANT: Embarrassing is the right word, son. This little sack of groceries is all that Pastor Pathetic's church was able to provide for our ministry to twenty widows in our community. I got a chance to preach a night service there over six months ago. I bet two thousand people turned out. I preached about the King's love for orphans and widows and talked to them about our widow's ministry. I asked them to help with food and finances. One man cut me a check for fifty bucks and this sack of groceries is all they provided in six months.

PHANATIK: That's ridiculous. Four thousand members and they can only buy three cans of baked beans and a couple cans of tuna? That's sad!

KAI'RO: Yeah, but I bet they got some tight roller skates, homie!

STORYTELLER: All three burst into laughter.

KAI'RO: Look, I don't have a lot of money, but I appreciate what you're doin' in your town. Here's somethin' that will help maybe. Either way, I'm going to keep you in my prayers. Thanks for inspiring me and my man Phanatik here to keep bringing the Gospel to the streets.

STORYTELLER: Kai'Ro gave the Reverend a good bit of the money he had taken with him from the City of Doom. Phanatik did the same. The Reverend got a little misty-eyed and embraced them both.

REV. RELEVANT: If two men as young as you guys are willing to walk the path of the King with the boldness you just demonstrated back there it gives me great hope. You two are the inspiration. The King told Peter that the church would kick in the very gates of Hell. If the King raises up more soldiers like you it's only a matter of time before those gates come crashing down!

STORYTELLER: The three put their arms around each other in a small circle and prayed. They shook hands and then Kai'Ro and Phanatik went on their way down the Heavenly Highway.

CHAPTER THIRTEEN:
THE CITY OF
BABEL-BLING

STORYTELLER: After saying goodbye to Reverend Relevant the two companions continued on their journey. Before long they saw a familiar face approaching them. It was the Preacher.

KAI'RO: Hey, Preacher! it's good to see you.

PREACHER: Likewise. I see that you two finally met up. That's good news.

PHANATIK: Yeah, we've been enjoying doing this thing together. Two are certainly better than one. That's for sure.

PREACHER: Yes indeed. Listen, I was hoping to catch up with both of you. I know that you've been through a whole lot already. I'm proud of your progress.

KAI'RO: Yes, sir. It hasn't been easy. I mean I'm not goin' to lie. There's been several times I wanted to quit.

PREACHER: Well, you've made it this far, and that's wonderful news. But I must warn you that you are going to be entering even greater trials still.

PHANATIK: What do you mean?

PREACHER: Not far from here is a great city called the City of Babel-Bling. It's probably the oldest city in the world. You two must pass through there on your way. Most of those who live there are not friendly with the King's soldiers. In fact, most of them hate the King. I wish I could promise you a safe trip, but I can't. I told both of ya'll that there would be trouble and danger on this road, and you've already experienced that personally.

PHANATIK: Yes sir, we have. I knew what I was getting into. I hope the King gives us the strength we'll need no matter what comes our way.

PREACHER: If you trust in the King with all your heart, He will not disappoint you or fail you. Hold fast to his promises. Cling to His Word.

KAI'RO: Thanks for the heads up Preacher.

PREACHER: Go now my sons, and may the King go with you.

STORYTELLER: Kai'Ro and Phanatik said goodbye to the Preacher and walked on together for a while. Then, in my dream I saw an enormous city just like the Preacher had told them. It stretched out almost as far as the eye could see. There were tall skyscrapers that shot high like towers and there were malls and shopping centers scattered everywhere. The buildings had a shine to them as if they were made out of diamonds. Yet, despite the glow, there was a dull grey smog that draped over the city like a dirty blanket. Flashy billboards were all along the road as the two travelers got closer. They had pictures of everything a man or woman could ever want—cars, jewelry, and clothing. As the men walked into town they were amazed to see how crowded it was. There were people in the streets, shouting, and bumping into one another. People were dressed in all kinds of ways. Some looked like thugs, others like pimps and hustlers, and then there were men and women dressed in pricey business suits. They were in and out of the stores buying and selling and making a great stir. When Kai'Ro and Phanatik entered into town a lot of the people stopped to stare. They had rarely seen guys dressed like them. Some people looked at them with big frowns on their faces. Plenty of people laughed at them and called them some terrible names. A few rough looking guys even came up to Phanatik and shoved him to the ground real hard. They balled up their fists expecting a fight, but Phanatik just got back on his feet. Kai'Ro put his arm on his friend and the two continued to press forward. As they went, people hollered at them and asked them where they were from. They told them as kindly as they could that they were pilgrims and strangers in this place—they were just passing through on their way to the City of Gold. When they said this, almost everyone laughed and started to curse at them again. and call them names. The whole time this was going on, people were getting in Phanatik and Kai'Ro's faces, waving their goods and begging them to buy the things they were selling. One woman brought out a handful of shiny silver chains and told them how tight they would look if they bought them. Another man dangled the keys to a nice car in front of them. He promised that they would get all the ladies if they just bought one of his rides. A few rough looking guys ran up to them and offered them some drugs. Others tried to sell them music, shoes, and even some beautiful looking girls promised them pleasure upon pleasure. Yet every time someone brought them another item they turned away and set their focus on the road ahead. Kai'Ro and Phanatik refused to enter any of their stores or shopping centers. Both felt drawn by different things, but both resisted by reminding each other that none of these things satisfy. As peacefully and gently as they could they engaged different people down the streets in conversation. They tried to tell them about the treasures of the King and his City of Gold. A few people would listen, but most people tuned them out and then cussed them out. I could tell that Kai'Ro and Phanatik were growing weary with everything that was being shoved in their faces. Finally, Phanatik hollered out:

PHANATIK: Look ya'll, we don't *want* what you're sellin'! You feel me? We want the Truth!

STORYTELLER: As soon as he said this the streets got quiet for a moment and everyone turned to face the two visitors. Pushing through the crowd came a group of large bouncers from a club called Do-It-In-the-Dark. Their leader was a strong man named No-Mercy.

NO-MERCY: What'cha talkin' about when you say *"the Truth,"* fool? You think you got something we don't got? You sayin' that all this stuff we got goin' on in Babel-Bling is a lie or somethin' punk? Say somethin' before I knock your face in.

STORYTELLER: The group of bouncers and several of the people and store owners gathered around Kai'Ro and Phanatik until there was hardly any space for them to move. No-Mercy got right up in Phanatik's face until their noses were almost touching. His eyes were full of a deep hate, the kind that can snuff a man's life out and never think another thing about about it.

PHANATIK: (with courage) All I'm sayin' to ya, brotha,' is that if you and the rest of the people in Babel-Bling think that the stuff you're sellin' and what you got goin' on here is somehow the "real life" then you're in bondage to a lie. The power and the pleasure that ya'll are pawnin' off here is a joke in comparison to what the King has to offer. Only the King and His Kingdom can offer a brotha the real life.

STORYTELLER: The whole crowd started shouting and waving their hands at them. A few thugs started throwing things at them. Without warning, No-Mercy punched Phanatik in the face with a punch that could have knocked a tree over. Phanatik went flying back into the crowd and went limp because that blow almost knocked the life out of him. Kai'Ro turned to help his friend but some of the bouncers and people in the crowd grabbed him and tossed him to the side. No-Mercy grabbed Phanatik by the throat and hit him two more times until Phanatik fell to the ground in a heap. At this point the mob grew crazed like sharks when there's blood in the water. Several people, including some of the women, started kicking Phanatik and hitting him. Kai'Ro shook free from the hands and feet holding him down and pushed his way through the crowd. Finally, he was able to crawl on top of his fallen friend and take some of the blows. He cried out in agony as they gave him a savage beating. I thought for sure that both of them would die. Then I heard some loud whistles and two men with badges, dresssed in camouflage, burst onto the scene. They started knocking the mob back with their clubs. One of the men was named Corruption and the other was No-Justice. After striking several of the people around them senseless, they cleared a path to Kai'Ro and Phanatik. Both of them were unconscious and bleeding terribly. The two men stopped. But instead of doing anything to help, they just smiled.

CORRUPTION: Now what in the world happened here to these two guys?

NO-MERCY: Those two fools came into this town and started a riot.

NO-JUSTICE: A riot?

NO-MERCY: Yeah, that's right. They came in here talkin' all this noise about how they were just passin' through on to some City of

Gold or somethin'. Everywhere they went they kept yappin' 'bout this King of theirs and how tight He was, and all that. They said they were too good for our sorry town. When some of the folks tried to offer them somethin' to buy or do, they'd just turn away. They came in here all crazy. I mean look at 'em with that weird armor they got on. They're clowns, dawg. With all that noise they were talkin' 'bout their City of Gold and all that nonsense…man… it got some of us fired up. When that idiot there said he wanted the Truth and that we was all livin' and believin' a lie well…I just snapped.

CORRUPTION: Looks like we've got some trouble with these two. We got 'em on a count of questioning the Code of Babel-Bling. We got 'em on disturbing the peace of our town.

NO-JUSTICE: And we got 'em on tellin' people lies and then startin' a riot.

CORRUPTION: I'd like to just leave 'em here, but this mob will tear 'em apart.

NO-JUSTICE: Let's haul their sorry butts to the Cage. Let's give 'em a trial before Judge Hate-Good and see what happens.

STORYTELLER: The two men dragged Kai'Ro and Phanatik through the road into the center of town. They were tossed into two rusted cages like animals. The cages were full of garbage and dried blood. They smelled horrible. Many people from the town continued to point at them and mock them. Some hurled bottles at the cages and glass shattered all over their bloodied bodies. Both of them had regained consciousness, but they could hardly shield their bodies from the glass and objects thrown at them. On occasion a few people spoke up and shouted at the crowd. They claimed that Kai'Ro and Phanatik had done nothing wrong. Whenever these people spoke, the crowd cussed them out. Some of them were slapped around and threatened that they'd be thrown in the Cage too if they didn't shut their mouths. Within a short period of time another riot almost broke out as the crowds turned on one another kicking, punching, and fighting. Several officers from Corruption and No-Justice's squadron flailed into the crowd again, beating them back with their clubs and ordering everyone to calm down. Just then there was a loud crash like thunder. The crowd grew still and looked up. High above them in an old stone tower was a tall thin man. He was dressed in black from head to toe. In his hands was a twisted cane with a shiny red skull on the top. His face was shriveled up like a prune and his eyes were hidden behind thick sunglasses. He was Judge Hate-Good and this was his city.

HATE-GOOD: Silence, you ridiculous fools! Why is there such nonsense going on in my town again? Can you not see that we have the two visitors in the Cage? Do not worry about them any longer. They are in our hands now and they will receive the justice that is coming to them.

STORYTELLER: A young man in the crowd below named Hopeful shouted out that they had done nothing wrong and that they should be set free. One of Corruption's officers clubbed him from behind and he fell.

HATE-GOOD: These men will receive a trial for their crimes against our town. We are just. They will receive what is coming to them and it will be justice indeed. Arrange the court.

STORYTELLER: Five wooden chairs were pulled out for five older gentlemen. Like Judge Hate-Good they carried the crooked canes with the red skulls. Their names were Bondage-Maker, Lord-Greed, Bloodsport, Death Dealer, and Lord-Liar. All of them glared at Kai'Ro and Phanatik who were still in the corners of their cages. As they were seated, Phanatik crawled to the edge of his cage and with a groan of pain pulled himself up onto his feet.

HATE-GOOD: Do we have witnesses against these men?

CORRUPTION: We do, sir. Our first witness is the owner of Poison Pawn Shop. His name is Tight Fist.

STORYTELLER: Corruption had Tight Fist place his hand and swear on a book with a picture of a woman riding a large and ugly red beast.

TIGHT FIST: Yes, I got somethin' to say about these two. They came talkin' about how all the stuff that we're sellin' in Babel-Bling is goin' to burn one day. They said that we were sellin' and hoardin' up treasure that wasn't goin' to last. In fact, that one Phanatik said that we were worshipin' idols and givin' up our souls in exchange for pleasure and treasure. He said that if we put our hope in these things that we'd eventually find out that they were hopeless, and that those things would leave our souls when it counted most for eternal punishment. Who does he think he is? This city has been offerin' the stuff he's hatin' on for as long as it's been around. Don't know about ya'll, but I'm *more* than happy with what Babel-Bling has to offer!

STORYTELLER: Most of the people shouted out their agreement and others picked up things to throw at the cages.

HATE-GOOD: His words are those of a trouble-making fool. They should be thrashed again just for saying something so stupid and false. Call forward the next witness. We will build our case against them.

CORRUPTION: Out next witness is Twilight. She works at the strip-club, Pleasure Trap.

STORYTELLER: Twilight swore on the book.

TWILIGHT: Yeah, these guys was tellin' me that I had no business doin' what I was doin'. They said that the King made me in His image and that He didn't want me usin' my body for somethin' trashy like dancin'. Last I checked...my body's been mine! They said that I was blinded by our lord of this town, Diablo, and that he had me trapped in a lie—a lie that I could use my body anyway I pleased as long as it paid the bills. They told me that this King of theirs made me and my body and that *He* owned it and not me! They even said that *none* of us really owned our bodies and that we had no right to do with it whatever we wanted. I heard 'em say that the idea that our bodies are our own is a lie from Hell and that Diablo's a son of Hell. In fact, they said that I was 'sposed to use my body for this King's glory! Can you believe that? Then, they started sayin' our hearts are always searchin' for pleasure but that the pleasure we're searchin' for is in all the wrong places, and that they won't last. One of 'em said that only the King could give us pleasure for real and that anything else that we were chasin' or doin' that didn't have to do with that King of theirs was totally meaningless and empty. Trust me…when I dance there's a lot of guys that get pleasure…that's what I do, and yeah, I'm good at it. Who are these two clowns to tell me that my body is some treasure of a King and that He made me to use it for His glory? They're craaazy!

HATE-GOOD: All these lies! Corruption, it's a wonder that you let these men live. I have never heard such filth! Are there any more witnesses?

CORRUPTION: Yes sir, there is another. His name is Crafty and he a professor at the University of Random Truths.

STORYTELLER: Like the two before him, Crafty swore with his hand on the evil book.

CRAFTY: Yes, I was amazed at the lies these young men spoke. There has always been a sense of order in our lovely city until these two came along. We learned to tolerate one another and to respect one another's different truths. Our town has always believed that there is no absolute truth but that we all can live by our own personal truth. Is it not a fact that each of us have found our pleasure, purpose, and happiness by discovering our own truth? Yet, these men said that there is an absolute Truth that is greater than all other truths. They said to me and others that the belief that all truths are okay is an illusion and a myth. They said that their King *was* the Truth and that the Truth of His Word had set them free! They said that the truths that we believed in—that life is ultimately about pleasure, about finding our own happiness, and about getting rich and being successful—were not *truths,* but were actually *lies.* They said that our University is a joke and that this whole town is a joke in comparison to the Kingdom of the King and the truths of His Kingdom. I heard them say that we are fools to be pitied if we believe that our town and what it has to offer is all that there really is.

HATE-GOOD: (shouting) Enough! I have heard enough of this trash. Do we even need another witness?

STORYTELLER: Phanatik grabbed the bars of the cage and shouted.

PHANATIK: If you are truly a believer in justice, you'll let us at least speak.

HATE-GOOD: If I had my way, I would kill you both now. But you are right. We will hear what you have to say and then we will give you the justice you deserve. Open the Cage and allow him to speak.

STORYTELLER: Phanatik limped forward. He was still bleeding and his face was bruised and swollen. I noticed that his armor, as real as it was, did not spare him from the brutal physical blows that these people had given him. He had one hand on his side holding his ribs. Though he was hurt badly, like a boxer after a one-sided fight, he stood bravely before the huge crowd.

PHANATIK: People of Babel-Bling, I hope that you'll listen to what I gotta say. I got truth for ya'll. I got somethin' that you just gotta hear! My name is Phanatik and I'm from the City of Doom. It wasn't that long ago that I felt the same way most of ya'll feel right now. I used to hate the King and everything He stood for. I mean when I heard people talk about Him and His words it used to make me sick. It seemed to me like He wanted to take all the fun out of life. It was rules, rules, rules. Besides that I didn't want anyone tryin' to call the shots in my life. I wanted to do my own thing, you know? I wanted to do what I wanted when I wanted. And for the longest that worked for me. I was a hustla'. I made for myself a lot of money and I was able to buy some of the nicer things. Beautiful girls used to crash in my crib. People on my block respected me, and my enemies stayed out of my way. I had everything this world had to offer. I was livin' large! But over time it started to lose its effect on me. I mean, it started gettin' harder and harder to feel good the way I wanted. I tried makin' more money. I tried buyin' more rides and even a bigger house. I found more girls and even started usin' some of the stuff I was sellin'. But it didn't work. Inside I felt like garbage. I got confused. Why wasn't this stuff makin' me happy no more? Some of you, if you look in your hearts, feel the same way. You're tired of this world and all it's lies. You're tired of chasin' after more and more stuff. Then, as soon as you get it, having it just vanish from ya hand like a cloud.

Well, I hit rock bottom for real. 'Bout that time I heard about the King. A Preacher told me that all that stuff I was doin' offended God, the One who made me. What he was sayin' started to click because I was already feelin' real down about all the people I'd hurt, the stuff I'd stolen, and the wicked things I'd done. Deep inside I felt real bad, you know? I felt hopeless for real. Then when the Preacher told me that I could have peace with God again if I'd give my life to the King, it gave me real hope. You see, even though I had all those things, I had no hope. In fact, I was hopeless. Lonely. Scared. I'd go to bed some nights and just cry when no one was lookin' or listenin'. It was a big decision for me, but I said goodbye to all the hustlin' and crime. I told some of my homies goodbye too. It was huge, but I learned that there was treasure in heaven, in the King's City of Gold. It was treasure that would give peace—peace that would last for my whole life. This sounded so good to me because all the treasure I had already stored up for myself didn't satisfy me at all.

So what Tight Fist told ya'll 'bout what I said is true for the most part. If ya'll are puttin your hope in the treasures of this world, I'm sorry, but they're going to pass and you're gonna pass away with 'em. You can't take none of this stuff with you. Only the King and His Kingdom last forever. I decided to flip the script in my life and start chasin' the treasure of the King because I knew that would last. I don't want to sound like I'm hatin' but this sorry town is sellin' everybody here a pack of lies. I would beg you not to let this place become your home. My boy, Kai'Ro, and I realized that this whole world ain't our home no more. I mean we live here, but the day we gave our lives to the King, that's the day we became citizens of a new family and new country.

And what Twilight said about me is mostly true too. God made each one of us. We ain't no accident. So if you're strippin' in clubs, takin' drugs, gettin' drunk, or just tryin' to find the next fix for your body to make it feel good, then you're doin' wrong. I mean I can't be more plain than that. The King made each of us for His glory. He gave us talents and abilities so that we could use them for His glory. Take me for instance. The King gave me the ability to be a good businessman. I mean I had mad skills back when I was a shortie at just makin' money. But when I got a little older I started usin' those skills for evil stuff. I learned that I could make a dime a whole lot quicker if I started dealin' and hustlin'. It didn't take long before I was one of the richest guys in town. I was listenin' to my own sinful heart and to the lies of Diablo. Don't listen to the lies of Diablo! The prince of this town is a fork-tongued snake that deserves nuttin' but Hell! He keeps tryin' to convince all of us that our appetites and our desire for pleasure are all that really matter, but that ain't true. We aren't going to find pleasure and happiness until we give our lives to the King! Let me put it to you like this... when you get tired and thirsty you go out and buy a sports drink to quench your thirst, right? Well, chasin' pleasures is like chasin' sports drinks. I mean, they'll satisfy you for a moment, but then you gotta get another one the next time you get thirsty. When you get with the King, *He* fills you up and you don't thirst no more. His Kingdom satisfies you. When I gave my life to Him it was like I didn't need all the other things no more. He became all I needed.

Lastly, I'd like to say somethin' about what Crafty said. Crafty and the dudes like him are all liars. They say that there's all kinds a truths out there when it comes to right and wrong and that any one of 'em will lead you to happiness. Don't buy that! The King said that there's only one Truth and He's it! If you don't have Him then you got nothin'. You'll find yourself holdin' on to an idea or a belief that's really just a lie. It might work for you for a while, but it ends in death. There are lots of ways that seem right to man, but they all end in death if they don't line up with the King and what He has to say. I'm cryin' out to ya'll! Hear what I gotta say. Don't settle for what this place is tellin' you and what it's sellin' you. You too can find peace, hope, joy, and life everlasting if you'll just get outta here and get on the Heavenly Highway. I know some of ya'll hear me...

HATE-GOOD: That's enough! We've heard enough of your garbage. There's no use listening to any more of his pathetic ideas. Do we even need to meet and discuss their verdicts?

BONDAGE MAKER: No. I have no need to discuss anything. If trash like these kids don't want the freedom and life that this town has to offer, then they don't need to be alive at all. Guilty!

LORD-GREED: If they don't want to get all that they can out of this world, then why be alive at all? I'm embarrassed that we even let him speak! Guilty on every charge!

BLOOD-SPORT: I would like to see the blood of their bodies spilled on the streets as an example to anyone who dares to believe their lies. *Guilty!*

DEATH-DEALER: Let them die for blaspheming the name of our lord Diablo and for humiliating our city! If there were more youth like them, can you imagine what would happen to our world? It would fall apart!

LORD-LIAR: I have no patience for pretenders and con-artists. Their lies made my ears burn and to look at them makes me sick. I have no doubt that they both are guilty.

STORYTELLER: Kai'Ro stood up in his cage when he heard all their verdicts. Phanatik never flinched or even looked down. Instead he stared each of them in the eyes. In my dream it appeared that a shaft of white light began to shine faintly around him.

HATE-GOOD: There you have it. We have a decision of justice just as I said we would. These sightless boys had the nerve to call us blind. These liars claimed we didn't know the truth. They told us that we were in bondage and yet they ended up in the Cage. What a funny twist! I believe that the only fitting punishment for these two fools is death. Prepare this one for execution. We will hear him cry out for mercy. But he won't find any.

PHANATIK: I have no fear of you or of these men. It's well with my soul. You, however, should fear the One who has the power to throw your body and your soul into Hell.

HATE-GOOD: (waving his hand) Finish him off!

STORYTELLER: Corruption, No-Mercy and the other officers rushed forward with their clubs and what I saw in my dream caused my heart to break. Those men beat poor Phanatik mercilessly until he dropped to the ground. Then they kicked and beat him when he was down. Kai'Ro grabbed the bars of his cage and shook them and cried out, but they would not listen. Though the sounds of their clubs on his body was sickening with every blow, Phanatik's face was covered with a mysterious peace. He was lying on his back with his eyes fixed towards heaven and the faint light around him grew brighter and brighter until those in the crowd and those with clubs had to squint. His lips were moving and I heard him say: "Unless a seed falls to the ground and dies, it remains alone; but if it dies it bears much fruit…"

After several minutes of beating him until he was almost unrecognizable, Hate-Good came down from his tower with a large gun in his hands. The gun had the words *Worldly Judgment* on it. He pointed it at Phanatik and fired off one sharp shot. Phanatik lay still. He was dead. Hate-Good turned to Kai'Ro's cage and snarled.

HATE-GOOD: Do you see what happened to your friend here? He opened his mouth and filled our town with his filth. You would do well to learn from his mistakes. The City of Babel-Bling shows love to those who love it back, but we hate with all our souls those who follow this King of yours! I think everyone here has learned a lesson today. Do two need to die? Perhaps. Take this man out and thrash him within an inch of his life, and toss him out of town. I don't think he'll come this way again.

STORYTELLER: With that, Hate-Good returned to the stairwell and climbed back up his tower. Corruption and the others pulled Kai'Ro from the Cage and like Phanatik, they gave him a fierce beating with their clubs. True to their orders, they beat him until he was nearly dead. Then they dragged him out of town and dumped his body along the side of the road. Kai'Ro laid there in a heap and did not move. But in my dream I saw one wandering from out of the city. He came out on the road. He was creeping carefully through the shadows. When he came up close to Kai'Ro's body, I could see that it was Hopeful.

CHAPTER FOURTEEN:
HOPEFUL

STORYTELLER: The night was very dark, and in my dream I saw flashes of lightening. I also heard loud thunder. A fierce rain started to fall. Hopeful stooped down beside Kai'Ro and tried to wake him, but Kai'Ro barely had breath left in him.

HOPEFUL: Dang, they messed you up bad, dawg. I gotta get you to the doctor.

STORYTELLER: Hopeful hoisted Kai'Ro up over his shoulder with a great heave. Then he went sloshing down the path as the rain continued to pour and the lightening flashed all around him. Hopeful went on like this for miles, carrying Kai'Ro because he couldn't carry himself. Finally a small house appeared on the side of the road. When the lightning flashed, I could see a mailbox that read: "Dr. Mercy."

HOPEFUL: Man, I hope the Doc is up, 'cause this boy might not make it.

STORYTELLER: Hopeful made it up to Dr. Mercy's front door and rang the bell. A light came on inside and the door was thrown open. I saw a woman wrapped in a white robe with white slippers on her feet. She was an older woman, but she had a beautiful glow to her face. Her hair was pulled up in a bun. She looked concerned.

MERCY: Oh, my! What has happened to your friend here?

HOPEFUL: Judge Hate-Good and his men beat this brother half to death.

MERCY: For *what*?

HOPEFUL: For nothin' really.

MERCY: He must have had issues with the fact that this young man is one of the King's servants. Won't you come in?

HOPEFUL: (entering the house and setting Kai'Ro on a couch) How'd you know he was one of the King's servants?

MERCY: It's obvious, honey. Look at his armor. Look at his mark. These things stand out if you have eyes to see. Was there no one with him? It's a dangerous road for a soldier to enter Babel-Bling alone.

HOPEFUL: No, he had another brotha with him named Phanatik. They killed him. Phanatik spoke like no one I've heard before. He spoke like he and the King were best friends…it was like this whole world had nothin' to offer him. It was like he knew he was going to die for the King and that didn't bother him at all. I've seen a lot of rough thugs in my life, but I've never seen a guy as brave as him.

STORYTELLER: While Hopeful was speaking, Mercy went to a cabinet and pulled out some bandages and ointments. I saw that one of the bottles of ointment was labeled Compassion and the other was called Grace. Mercy washed Kai'Ro's wounds and cleaned them with the ointments.

HOPEFUL: I'm sorry, ma'am, but I don't have no money to pay for any of this…

MERCY: Please, son, it's a joy to take in two strangers. If you'd like, there's still some soup on the stove.

HOPEFUL: I appreciate it, but I'm all right. I'd like to just sit here, if that's OK?

MERCY: How old are you, son?

HOPEFUL: I'm fifteen, ma'am.

MERCY: Kind of young to be carrying a battered man around in the dead of night, aren't you? Bet your mom's worried about you?

HOPEFUL: Naw, not really.

MERCY: Every mom worries, son.

HOPEFUL: Not my mom. She ran out on me about five years ago. I haven't seen her for the longest.

MERCY: And your father?

HOPEFUL: He's been locked up since before I was born...killed somebody or somethin'...I don't know.

MERCY: No family?

HOPEFUL: Yeah, if you're countin' the streets as family. Then I got a whole bunch of family.

MERCY: You don't have a single brother or sister....nothing at all?

HOPEFUL: My brother's dead. He got shot. My sister has got like three kids from three different men and lives somewhere over there in Shametown...I don't know. I haven't seen her in the longest either. Like I said, I got some brothas on the streets...we've been together...and we're pretty tight.

MERCY: The streets are no kind of family, son. I'm sorry you don't have any flesh and blood to take you in.

HOPEFUL: That's okay...I guess I've just always felt in my heart that things were gonna work out somehow. I've never felt like I just gotta give up or anything like that.

STORYTELLER: Mercy continued to bandage Kai'Ro and clean his wounds. It was a long job and Mercy worked tenderly and carefully. After a while Kai'Ro started to wake up. The ointments of Compassion and Grace had knocked down a lot of the swelling, and most of the minor cuts and bruises had almost gone away completely.

KAI'RO: Where am I?

HOPEFUL: We're at Mercy's house.

KAI'RO: Who are *you*?

MERCY: This is Hopeful. He's the young man who saved your life.

KAI'RO: For real? Thanks, brotha.

MERCY: You are fortunate, son, that Hate-Good did not kill you like your friend. It must have been the good graces of the King that you were spared.

KAI'RO: Yeah, well, I wish it *had* been me. My man, Phanatik, had so much courage out there. I was so scared inside. I could hardly say a word, but it was like he had the words for both of us. Now he's gone!

MERCY: The King takes all of us in our own time, son. Don't be mad because He took your friend and He left you behind. Phanatik fulfilled his purpose. The fact that you are still alive is no coincidence. Hate-Good spares no one. This must mean that the King is not finished with what He has for you just yet. You must continue to press into those plans for your life.

STORYTELLER: Kai'Ro's angry face started to soften. He did his best to sit up on the couch.

KAI'RO: So, Hopeful, what made you come and help me?

HOPEFUL: I guess it's 'cause I felt like you and Phanatik helped me first. I was on the corner at Death Drive when you and Phanatik started talking to some of the dealers on my block. They came at you tryin' to sell you some of their product. Those same guys recruited my older brother when he was about my age. He became one of their local dealers up and down Death Drive and over there along Addict Avenue. It wasn't more than about two months and my brother got shot dead. Well, they started recruiting me too. But when you two showed up and started talkin' about your King and His Kingdom it was like you were doing a whole different kind a recruitin'. The dealers, man, they're recruitin' kids to *die*. But you... you and Phanatik were recruitin' me and my boys to *life*. I could feel it stirring in me. A lot of guys my age are lookin' for hope in a bad kinda way. For most of us, the gang route and the drug route are the only ways out. But as for me, I've seen too many kids die, get messed up, and just disappear. That wasn't no kind of hope for me. Ya'll spoke with so much passion, dawg! I was just in total awe. I've heard guys talk with passion 'bout who they shot, which girl they got with, how much money they made and all that, but nobody has come on my corner talkin' that way about this King of yours. I guess for the first time I started to believe there was a way out for me…a *real* way out.

KAI'RO: Was that you that hollered out at Hate-Good?

HOPEFUL: (rubbing the knot on the back of his head) Yeah. That was me.

KAI'RO: Well, I appreciate what you did for me. I don't think I would have made it if you hadn't come to help me out.

MERCY: You would have died if it hadn't been for Hopeful.

HOPEFUL: It's no big deal. Like I said, I feel like you and Phanatik saved *my* life…so maybe we're even. So what's next for you?

KAI'RO: Same thing I been doing. I gotta get back on that Heavenly Highway.

HOPEFUL: Ya think I could roll with you…I mean I can't go back to Babel-Bling. I got no love for that place no more.

KAI'RO: You need to be in school, brotha. You're too young to be rollin' the streets with no real plans or nothin'. I know of a good school back in Struggletown. There's a man who runs a school down that way. He'd take you in and even give you a place to stay. You need an education. I dropped out when I was about your age, and I'm not proud of that decision. My brotha, Lil' One did the same thing and he's been walkin' a dangerous road just like you. Get you some education, some knowledge about the King's word. Reverend Relevant, the guy who runs that school, is a great man and he'll get you on the right path. That man doesn't just talk about the Gospel. He lives the Gospel by bringin' it to the streets.

HOPEFUL: That sounds good. I mean, if this Reverend will take me in I don't mind going back to school.

MERCY: That would be an excellent decision, young man. Your life isn't over just because you have no mom and no dad. That's a tragedy, but don't ever let that be an excuse. The King has plans for you, son, plans to prosper you and not to harm you...plans to give you both a hope and a future. He's had these plans for you since before you were born. You are still His child and He has wonderful things in store for you.

KAI'RO: Amen.

HOPEFUL: I've never really given up. I know what you're sayin' is true. I mean my life has been a mess and I've gone through some stuff, but I've always felt like I gotta hang on. A lot of folks in Babel-Bling just give up and check out. But I'm not there yet.

KAI'RO: Sometimes hope gives you just enough ability to hang on, but if you're hangin' on to the King and His word, then you're hangin' on to something that won't let you down...ever.

HOPEFUL: I feel you on that.

STORYTELLER: The three continued to talk for a while longer until Kai'Ro finally dozed off to sleep. Hopeful fell asleep in a chair and Mercy placed a blanket on him. She cleaned up a little bit and then walked over to a rocking chair by the window. Under a dim light she bowed her head and prayed for the two young men asleep in her living room.

CHAPTER FIFTEEN:
ON THE ROAD
AGAIN

STORYTELLER: Kai'Ro and Hopeful spent a few more days with Dr. Mercy. It didn't take long for the doctor's care to take effect. The bruises on Kai'Ro body healed quickly. Before long he was able to get back on his feet again and move around. During the days together, Kai'Ro wrote a letter for Hopeful to bring to Reverend Relevant. They talked a lot about the King and the Heavenly Highway. It finally came time for Kai'Ro to get back on the road.

KAI'RO: I need to thank both of you for puttin' me back together again. The King used you to save me. I owe you a lot of gratitude.

MERCY: No, I should be thanking you, my son. Seeing a young man like you with so much passion for the King and His ways does my heart so much good. I see so many hopeless young men and women walk by my place almost every day…most of them are just busy ruining their lives with violence, drugs, lying, and stealing. You don't see too many young soldiers like yourself. There's a lot of young people calling themselves soldiers and trying to act hard and trying to pretend that their street life is real life, but actually they're just living a dream.

HOPEFUL: Actually they're just livin' a *nightmare* and callin' it life. I gotta thank you too. Thanks for lettin' your faith shine like that for me in Babel-Bling. What you and Phanatik showed me was that real courage is actually rebellin' against this world and not conforming to it. I've seen cats take bullets and beatings out on the streets, but I've never seen nobody take a thrashin' for the King like that. And thanks for pointin' me to Reverend Relevant. You've helped give me a real shot in life.

STORYTELLER: The three took turns giving each other hugs. Then Hopeful said goodbye and took off with his letter from Kai'Ro.

MERCY: I saw what you did for that boy and I think the King is going to use you to reach a lot of these young people.

KAI'RO: What do you mean?

MERCY: You became a hero to Hopeful over the last few days. Now I'm not talking about the kind of hero you see on TV with

all the money and the celebrity and all that. Most of those people aren't heroes. He saw the life of the King inside of you and
it became something he wanted. He saw that you were walking
something that he had only heard other people talking about. That
made a powerful impact on him. I think the King is going to call you
back to where you came from…

KAI'RO: With all respect ma'am, I'm never going back to the City
of Doom. I *can't* go back that way again.

MERCY: I think you missed my meaning, son. It's obvious that
you're no longer the young man who once lived in that city. There's
no way you'd go back there and go back to your old ways. I believe
that. The city *needs* the life that you have. *That* is what I am saying. It needs a soldier to point the way to the Highway…to point
the way to the King. I have a feeling if you went back to your old
neighborhood they'd hardly recognize you. Sure, they'd recognize
your face, but they wouldn't recognize your soul. And your soul
says a whole lot more about you than anything else. Like Hopeful,
I think there's some young people who would listen. I think there's
a whole lot of folks that are thirsting inside for something that's
real…for hope…for life.

KAI'RO: I don't know, I guess I never really thought about it like
that. For me, I've just been trying to get to the City of Gold and just
make sure that I stay on that Heavenly Highway. Along the way I
figured I'd just tell people about the King.

MERCY: Well, that works, but I think the King may send you back
to your old city, your old block, and to your old friends. You need to
pray on it, because that may be what He has for you.

KAI'RO: Yes, ma'am. I'll pray on it. Thank you again. I best be
goin'.

STORYTELLER: Kai'Ro set out on the road again. As he moved
I could see a difference to him that was remarkable. His face was
alive with peace, wisdom, and strength. I no longer saw the fear
and insecurity that had been there before. His armor was dented
and banged up. There were scars on him. But he walked like a

warrior on a mission. To me, he seemed like a man from a whole different world altogether. After he moved on for a while I saw a gigantic tent off to the side of the road. It was gold and white, and from the top of the tent a flag was flapping in the wind with the words CIRCUS OF WISDOM on it. Kai'Ro stopped for a moment to see what was going on. Just outside the circus entrance was a tall and beautiful woman wearing a black top hat. She was older, but she was radiant looking. Her hair was long and pulled into a ponytail. She wore a flashy gold blouse with a flowing white cape that made her look like the Mistress of Ceremonies. She had a large megaphone held up to her mouth and she hollered to a large crowd gathered just outside of the CIRCUS.

SOPHIA: How long will you simple ones keep loving your simple ways? How long are you mockers going to keep on mocking? *Idiots!* How long will you refuse to learn? Turn to me and I can change your life! Look, I'm ready to pour out my spirit on you and tell you all I know. I've been calling you, but you walk right past as if you're deaf. When I've reached out to you, you just shove me away.

STORYTELLER: Most of the crowd ignored her. A few threw ugly hand gestures in her direction and others just laughed as she continued to cry out. Kai'Ro, who was curious, drew closer and started to push his way through the crowd. As he did so, Sophia shouted again.

SOPHIA: Since you laugh at what I'm saying and make jokes about my advice, how can I take you seriously? I'll turn the tables and joke about your troubles! What if the roof falls in, and your whole life goes to pieces? What if drama strikes and there's nothing to show for your life but rubble and ashes? You'll need me then. You'll call for me, but don't expect an answer. No matter how hard you look, you won't find me!

STORYTELLER: Kai'Ro had to push his way through the crowd. They were packed tightly. Many of those around him were sipping drinks out of paper bags. Some were arguing with one another. Others appeared to be gambling and fighting. As Kai'Ro drew up close to the tent's entrance Sophia saw him and smiled. It seemed like she had known he was coming.

SOPHIA: Traveler! Do you seek wisdom? Do you desire to gain insight on how to live your life? Would you like illumination to help you understand the world around you?

KAI'RO: Yes, ma'am. I would.

SOPHIA: Then you have come to the right place. There is so much to show you. Come inside with me.

STORYTELLER: She pulled back one of the large flaps and welcomed him into the tent. Inside was a shocking scene. The first room they entered was called PERSPECTIVE PLACE. It was a small room and there were several people walking around inside. But everything was upside-down and they were walking on the ceiling.

KAI'RO: Whoah! What's goin' on here?

SOPHIA: Strange, isn't it?

STORYTELLER: Kai'Ro stopped and rubbed his eyes to make sure he wasn't seeing things.

KAI'RO: Why are they all walking around in the air like that?

SOPHIA: Are you sure that *you're* not the one walking around in the air?

KAI'RO: Huh?

STORYTELLER: Kai'Ro looked down at his feet and saw that they were actually suspended in midair. His jaw dropped. He looked up at the people above him and saw that they were actually walking around on the ground.

KAI'RO: What in the world is goin' on here? Am I trippin' or something?

SOPHIA: No, sweetheart, you are learning your first valuable lesson. The wisdom of the King is from the Upside-Down Kingdom.

His ways are higher than our ways and His thoughts are higher than our thoughts. When you begin to see the world through the wisdom of the King, then everything around you looks like foolishness. But, you must also understand that if you walk by the King's wisdom *you* will also appear foolish to those who walk by the wisdom of the world.

STORYTELLER: Just then, those above him started to point at him and laugh. They made crude jokes about him and called him names.

SOPHIA: In the same way, the world mocked and persecuted the King when He walked the earth. They didn't understand Him or what He came to do. The King made it clear to His followers that just like the world misunderstood and hated Him, the world would misunderstand and hate everyone who followed Him.

KAI'RO: This just feels weird to me.

SOPHIA: It takes getting used to, but eventually you'll understand that what is right-side-up is actually upside-down. I'm sure you've already started to experience this on your journey.

KAI'RO: Yeah. When you mention it that way. I've talked to a lot of different folks, and many of 'em just don't seem to get it. I guess it's like what they're actually callin' truth and reality is in fact an illusion or something.

SOPHIA: Yes. Let me show you something else that may help you better understand this principle of upside-down being right.

STORYTELLER: Sophia took Kai'Ro into another part of the tent. They walked into a wide arena with a large sandy pit in the middle. The place was packed with people and Sophia sat down in one of the two remaining seats. She asked Kai'Ro to sit down next to her. Just then a large barrel-chested man came out into the center of the sand pit with a microphone. The arena went dark and only a bright spotlight shone down on the man in the center of the ring.

ANNOUNCER: Ladies and gentlemen...I present to you an amazing battle of overwhelming odds. You are about to witness something extraordinary. Hold your breath and do not be frightened as I unleash the gigantic...monstrous...bigger...than...life...killer... *Crusher!*

STORYTELLER: Just then the spotlight swung its beam to a part of the ring. A large metal door opened with a bang and a giant of a man came running out screaming. In his hands was a large Louisville slugger bat. He was nearly nine feet tall and every inch of his body was covered in rippling muscles. He roared and beat his chest with his hand. Many in the crowd shrieked and some even covered their eyes in fear.

KAI'RO: I've never seen a guy as big as that dude before...he's like a giant.

ANNOUNCER: And now...I present to you his competition...the humble...the tiny...the microscopic...the almost-so-small-you-might-miss-him...*Mighty Mite!!!*

STORYTELLER: The light swung again to another part of the ring and out of a small wooden door emerged a little man wearing some armor that appeared to be too big for him. He ran out into the ring with his little legs pumping as fast as they could go. He had a tiny shield with a large red Cross on it. In his hand was a tiny dagger. When he came into the center of the ring the crowd erupted into boos and people shook their heads in disbelief.

KAI'RO: Man, this is gonna be a slaughter...someone needs to get that lil' man out of there or they're going to be sending him home to his family in a soup can...

SOPHIA: Wait and see, child.

STORYTELLER: Crusher glared at Mighty Mite and his nostrils were flaring like a bull's before it charges. Mighty Mite closed his eyes and appeared to make a short prayer. Then he lowered the visor on his helmet.

ANNOUNCER: Let the battle begin!

STORYTELLER: Crusher let out another roar and took a great swing at Mighty Mite, but the little man rolled to the side and the bat swung over his body with a whoosh. Crusher cursed and pounded the bat into the ground again and again but Mighty Mite continued to roll ahead of his swings and out of harm's way. This went on for some time and the crowd grew restless and started chanting and booing again. Finally, Mighty Mite rose to his feet and dodged another great swing from the giant of a man. Crusher took another cut that could have knocked over a building but Mighty Mite ducked and rolled between his legs. Then with a quick stroke he stuck the giant in the rear-end with his dagger. Crusher howled and jumped in the air like a child who accidentally sat down on a bee. Several in the crowd burst into laughter. Crusher's eyes grew red as he looked at his tiny opponent with hatred. He gripped his bat with two hands and took another powerful swing, and to everyone's surprise Mighty Mite did not move. The bat struck him in the head with such force that the entire arena shook as if rocked by an explosion. Kai'Ro put his head in his hands.

KAI'RO: I can't watch this…

SOPHIA: (putting her hand on his shoulder) Look again, son.

STORYTELLER: Kai'Ro looked up slowly and could not believe what he saw. Mighty Mite was still standing in the same place and Crusher was holding the nub of a broken bat. The pieces of his slugger were all over the arena. Everyone in the audience was shocked. Crusher looked shocked as well. He snarled, balled up one of his mighty fists and punched it into Mighty Mite's chest. It was a blow that could break bricks. Instead, the arena was filled with the horrible sound of the bones in his hands being cracked and crushed to bits. Crusher screamed in pain. At this point the crowd began to cheer: *Might-ee Mite! Might-ee Mite*! This only made Crusher even more angry. With his good hand he tried to lift Mighty Mite off of the ground, but he couldn't. Frustrated, he kicked his tiny opponent. Once again, nothing happened except the crunching of his toes. Now he hopped around on one foot howling and yelling. The crowd burst into laughter and started cheering again. Crusher lost his balance and fell into the sand. Mighty Mite sprang onto Crusher's chest like a lion on its prey.

He raised his dagger for a finishing blow and the crowd urged him to finish the fight. They chanted: *Kill him! Kill him!* The little man thrust his blade down for a finishing blow, but just before he buried it in his chest the dagger burst into a beautiful bouquet of flowers. Mighty Mite held it high above his head in triumph and the crowd erupted into cheers that became almost deafening. Then the tiny man pointed towards heaven as the lights suddenly went out. As quickly as they went out they came on again, but when they did Kai'Ro was alone with Sophia in an empty arena.

SOPHIA: What did you see here, son?

KAI'RO: Well, I learned I need to get some of that lil' man's armor because that stuff is the real deal...Naw...I'm just playin'. I learned that the biggest and the baddest don't always win. That Crusher guy was the strongest and meanest man I've ever seen in my life. There was no way that he shoulda lost that fight...no way...

SOPHIA: So, how did he lose?

KAI'RO: He was too prideful...it was like he believed that just because he was bigger and stronger that he was guaranteed to win. He obviously didn't have what it takes even though it seemed like he did...even to me.

SOPHIA: And did Mighty Mite have what it takes?

KAI'RO: Yes, ma'am, he obviously had what it took to beat that monster...I mean...he took a savage beating...but the more he took the more it embarrassed and humiliated Crusher. It was like Crusher ended up looking like a complete fool in the end. I mean he got dogged out for real out there.

SOPHIA: The King uses the weak to shame the strong, and even things that are low and despised to shame the things that are high and mighty. Why do you think He does this?

KAI'RO: So no man can boast, I guess. I mean, Mighty Mite obviously had Someone bigger than him fightin' that battle for him because there's no way he should have won that one. No way.

SOPHIA: Kai'Ro, the world wants to impress upon you the power of human strength, riches, and success. The world continually boasts in what it has and what it does. But the King desires that you boast that you know Him and that you know He is living *in* and *through* you. This is your greatest boast. All of the King's servants are Mighty Mites. There are no super-servants that do anything great outside of what the King allows and provides on His own. The King shames the powers of this world by bringing those powers crashing down through the small and weak. Think about the little boy, David, who killed a giant like Crusher. The King himself took a small group of fishermen, tax collectors, a couple political hotheads, and He built a team that shook the earth. When the King writes a story He gets all the credit…that's because He's the King…He deserves it. He is a lover of impossible stories so that just like Mighty Mite's impossible victory over Crusher, we must sit back and say in awe, "Only the King could do that." When you seek to give Him the glory in all that you do, He will use you to topple the mighty and strong.

KAI'RO: That's deep.

SOPHIA: Yes, that's the Upside-Down Kingdom. The King uses midgets to knock down mountains, whispers to silence storms, and nobodies to change the world…

KAI'RO: Little nobodies like me?

SOPHIA: (smiling) Yes. Even little nobodies like you, son.

STORYTELLER: Just then there was a loud honking noise and a strange looking car drove out into the center of the sand pit. It was covered in all different colors as if someone had just taken different buckets of paint and sloshed them all over it. The wheels were all different sizes and they were wobbling as if they were about to come off. The car drove around in circles twice with a large plume of black smoke shooting out of the tailpipe. Then the car stopped and one of the side doors opened. A clown stepped out. On his head was a large orange wig with a funny hat sitting on top of it. He was wearing a bright red clown nose and his face was covered with white paint. His cheeks were round and rosy. He waddled out with big floppy shoes on, and he walked over to a small wooden chair in the center of the ring. Then, the clown sat down and pulled out a big Bible. He laid it down in his lap, and started to read. Just then a loud sound of bass came pounding into the arena as a black Bentley pulled into the ring. The glass was tinted dark, and it had sparkling silver rims. It circled around the clown and his little car once and then came to a halt. The doors were thrown open and four rough looking guys stepped out. They were all dressed in baggy jeans with long white tall-Ts. The driver, Flash, was smoking a large brown cigar. Shiny gold chains hung around their necks, and clean white and blue Air Force Ones were on their feet. They saw the clown reading his Bible. Flash pointed at him and took a step towards him.

FLASH: Yo, ya'll check out this clown here! I know him. He lives like three doors down from me…this punk is a loser for real!

STORYTELLER: The gang of thugs surrounded the clown and took turns harassing him.

THRILLS: What'cha doin', payaso? Sittin' there in that retarded outfit you got there, ese?

CASH: Look at this fool…just sittin' there like some kinda geek readin' that book of his.

ICE: I've never seen someone so stupid before.

STORYTELLER: The clown looked up at them for a moment, but then returned to reading his Bible.

THRILLS: (holding a bottle of Cerveza) Hey ese, why don't you come to any of the parties, payaso? I don't see you at none of the clubs. You one of them holy santos who's too good for everyone? Ain't you into the party scene…the girls, the Cerveza, the thrills, homie?

STORYTELLER: The clown looked up at Thrills and shook his head.

ICE: Why don't you have no nice clothes, homie? Dang! Ain't you got no ice, no shoes, no nothin'? You got anything nicer than that clown suit, fool? 'Cause that clothes you got on is lame!

STORYTELLER: The four young men burst into laughter. The clown shook his head again. Cash took out a wad of hundred dollar bills and ruffled them in the clown's face.

CASH: You got a stash like this clown? You got the green and the muscle to make things happen?

STORYTELLER: Again the clown just smiled and shook his head.

FLASH: (blowing smoke from his cigar) Naw, homies, he's got nothin'! He's just a clown…that's all…he's just a lame 'ole, Bible-followin', King-lovin', too broke, too lame, too gay, too weak, good-for-nothin' clown!

STORYTELLER: Flash pulled out a black gun from the back of his pants and held it up to the clown's head.

FLASH: Don't know 'bout ya'll, but I hate clowns! The world would be a better place without clowns like this fool.

STORYTELLER: He was about to pull the trigger, but just then a small fire engine burst into the arena with its sirens blaring. On the side of the fire engine were the words KING'S PERSPECTIVE. Flash and his crew looked at the fire engine in shock. Suddenly, the fire engine shot out a hard burst of water that doused them all. It was a powerful blast and for a while Kai'Ro couldn't see what was going on. After the mist cleared and the fire engine drove away there was a new scene before him. There was a young man who looked a whole lot like Kai'Ro sitting on the bench with his Bible. He had on jeans and a t-shirt. A simple cross hung from his neck. Around the bench were four clowns. They were dumpy and goofy looking clowns. Their crisp jeans and fresh Ts were replaced with skin-tight polka dot pants and fluffy-frilly polka dot shirts. On their feet were Air Force Ones, but they were fat and floppy with bright pink shoelaces. The jewelry around their necks was big, clunky plastic with rocks inside. It was so heavy that it nearly pulled them over.

THRILLS: (holding a baby bottle) Man, what happened to us, ese?

STORYTELLER: Ice tried to say something but there was a huge pacifier in his mouth. Flash looked at his hand and saw that he was holding a big plastic gun that shot bubbles. Cash glanced at his wad of money and was shocked to see a handful of large Monopoly game bills.

CASH: Man, I'm flat broke, homie. This won't buy me nothin'.

FLASH: (puffing on his cigar and looking at his bubble gun) Shoot, this ain't right, ya'll. This ain't right!

STORYTELLER: Just then Flash's cigar exploded with a crack and covered his face with soot.

FLASH: Man, let's get outta here, dawg. This is crazy.

STORYTELLER: The four of them waddled as fast as they could back to their Bentley, but the Bentley was gone. What was left was a rusted and ugly bicycle with four seats on it.

THRILLS: I ain't fixin' to ride on that thing, homie.

FLASH: Man, get your butt on that bike. We gotta get out of here!

STORYTELLER: The four clowns jumped on the bike and pedaled away. The tires on the bike were very wobbly and the clowns crashed three times before they finally made it to a tunnel and disappeared.

KAI'RO: Why do the nations conspire and the people plot in vain?

SOPHIA: …The kings of the earth take their stand and the rulers gather together against the King and against His Anointed One…

KAI'RO: The One enthroned in heaven *laughs*; the King laughs at these clowns until his stomach hurts…

SOPHIA: This is good. You know the King's Letters. Most of the world calls the King's followers clowns, and they do everything to make fun of the King's people. They think that those who identify with the King and take His ways seriously are no better than fools…

KAI'RO: Yeah, but the King makes the final call. Anyone who starts cheering about *this* world and the power and pleasure it offers is the *clown!* That type of person is fooled. We've got clowns on the radio, clowns in the videos, clowns signing record deals, and clowns in the movies.

SOPHIA: But again it's only in the Upside-Down Kingdom that you can see that they're the clowns. These clowns try to mask their foolishness behind sunglasses, jewelry, expensive cars , videos, parties and clothing. But the King is coming back! And when He does, He will strip them of all their imaginary power and reveal them to every one around as clowns. What a sad and humiliating day that will be! Come on, there is still more to see.

STORYTELLER: Sophia took Kai'Ro by the hand and led him into another part of the Circus. In this next room there was a tall man with a long mustache. He had on bright suspenders and a bowler hat. On his suspenders was a button that said: MR. OPPORTUNITY. In front of him was a large crowd of people from all over the world. They were gathered and waiting. Behind him and to his left were three booths and to his right was a large open plot of ground that looked like a garden

MR. OPPORTUNITY: Step right up, ladies and gentlemen! Don't be shy! Come here, get your LIFE and get ready to use it any way you please!

STORYTELLER: The eager crowd filed into a large line and Mr. Opportunity handed each of them a green ticket with the word LIFE on it. Every single person received one ticket. Behind Mr. Opportunity were more vendors who hollered to the crowds. To his left were "bottle toss" booths. One booth was called the Blame Booth. One was called The Booth of Entitlement, and the last one was called The Booth for Quick Fixes. The people operating these booths were sneaky looking and they hollered to the crowd as soon as they came in with their LIFE ticket.

VENDOR ONE: Come to the Blame Booth. Have you had a hard life? Maybe a no-good family? You have a horrible job? Perhaps you've grown up in a bad neighborhood or go to a really bad school! Or wait…maybe you're a victim of the government or of an unfair system. Step up to my booth, ladies and gentlemen! Give me your LIFE and I'll give you one shot…one lucky shot. We have terrific door prizes that we're just giving away, so come on! What'cha say…give me your LIFE and give it a toss!

VENDOR TWO: Ladies and gentlemen, step up to the Booth of Entitlement! Do you have unresolved problems? Are people not meeting your needs? Who's going to solve your issues? Why is no one giving you what's yours? Who's putting unrealistic expectations on you? Give me your LIFE and I will give you one toss. You won't believe the door prizes I have waiting for you.

VENDOR THREE: Who needs a Quick Fix? Do you sir? Surely you do ma'am! Line up! Line up! That's it! That's it! Give me your LIFE! This is a no-brainer. I'll give you one shot! You knock down the bottles and I'll give you all kinds of pleasures and thrills. There's no need to strain or struggle for anything. Just give me your LIFE and I guarantee you will walk away with something grand!

STORYTELLER: All three booths had large, fat bottles that almost anyone could hit. It looked like an easy game. Many of those with their LIFE tickets started to line up at the various booths as the Vendors continued to holler at them to come and spend their LIFE. There was no real rhyme or reason to who lined up because I saw people from every race and language. There were the rich and poor, the clothed and nearly naked. To the right an old man in overalls named Farmer Diligence hollered to those with their LIFE tickets to step up and buy a bag of seeds. Above his head was an old wooden sign that said, THE GARDEN OF COMMUNITY AND RESPONSIBILITY.

FARMER DILIGENCE: Give me your LIFE and I'll give you a bag of seeds. You can come, step up into the Garden, dig in the dirt, plant your seeds, and watch 'em grow. It's a long term investment, but I promise you there'll be fruit for ya. Don't waste your life blamin' people, tryin' to get others to do for you what you should do for yourself, or seekin' a quick fix for somethin' that won't last.

STORYTELLER: A few people stopped and some even exchanged their LIFE ticket for a small sack of seeds, a shovel, and a watering can. Many of those in the crowd who were trying to make up their mind looked back at the booths once they saw that the people in the Garden were having to do some really hard work. Some mumbled that the booths seemed much easier and made more sense. I saw in my dream that almost everyone who threw one of the balls at the bottles hit the mark and sent the bottles soaring with a great crash. Every time they exploded, the crowd roared in excitement. The Vendors filled the winners' hands with shiny tokens. On each token was written with different words: FLEETING PLEASURE, UNEARNED WAGES, SMALL COMFORT, MEANINGLESSNESS, BITTERNESS, and FRUSTRATION. The winners took little time to really *look* at the tokens. The Vendors asked them to move to another booth called the Payout Booth in the back corner. There, they could cash in their tokens for their door prize. They went with excitement on their faces and handed their coins to the Payout Clerk. She smiled at them, reached behind a counter and pulled out a wilted and dying potted plant. Each winner received one. But each one who received the prize protested. The Clerk laughed at them and told them that they got just what they deserved.

CLERK: What did you expect you sad fools? Did you really think that gambling your LIFE away on Blame, Entitlement, and Quick Fixes would somehow win you something special? I'm sorry, but a LIFE wasted on those things will be fruitless and dead.

STORYTELLER: One at a time the winners slowly walked away. Some went away crying. Others went away cursing. Still others just sat down and stared at the useless plant in their hands.

KAI'RO: Shoot! That's messed up! Those poor people got hoodwinked and now they got nothin' to show for it.

SOPHIA: Yes, Kai'Ro, it's a horrible ending to a wasted LIFE, but those poor people reaped what they sowed. Take another glance at the Garden.

STORYTELLER: Back at the Garden something interesting was happening. Those who had tilled the soil, planted, and watered their seeds were all staring at the ground. All of them were sweaty and dirty. I noticed how each of them had aged to varying degrees. As they were staring at the ground little green shoots started to push up through the soil. They grew quickly until each of them became gorgeous looking trees. The limbs were full of pretty flowers and lush fruits. All the people cheered and hugged one another. As they pulled the fruits from the limbs there were different words on each piece. There were words like HOPE, PURPOSE, MEANING, DAILY BREAD, PEACE and DIRECTION. The fruit looked delicious, and those in the Garden took the whole day to enjoy it. Then, to my surprise, one person with all the fruit noticed the crowd of people outside who were stuck with their dead plants. He motioned to those in the Garden and they started grabbing armfuls of the fruit, offering HOPE, PURPOSE, MEANING, DAILY BREAD, PEACE, and DIRECTION to those who had nothing. Some of those who had wasted their LIFE at the booth gladly and joyously took the fruit, but others shoved it away and clung to their dead plant as if they were proud of it.

SOPHIA: Do you understand the meaning of all this, Kai'Ro?

KAI'RO: Whew! There's a lot going on here…but I'll give it a shot. Everyone gets a LIFE. We all got that in common…and LIFE is an *opportunity*. Even though we all get a LIFE our lives aren't all the same. When I saw that crowd I saw people from everywhere. There were some who looked like they hadn't eaten in weeks, and there were some who looked like they hadn't *stopped* eating in weeks. I saw bums and I saw millionaires. There were people who talked educated and people who talked like they hadn't seen a day in school. I guess everybody had an opportunity to spend their LIFE on something. Seemed to me like the people who wanted the least amount of struggle chose those booths. They thought it'd be easier to blame folks and try to get some quick results.

SOPHIA: Why is that such a temptation, and why do you think most people chose those booths?

KAI'RO: Well...I mean it's just that most people are gonna take the easy road. Besides...hittin' those bottles was a surefire thing... a baby could hit those bottles. I remember growin' up as a kid that I used to blame just about everyone and everything for my problems. Even when I got in trouble it was somebody else's fault. It felt better when you could convince yourself that your problems weren't your fault. And quick fixes...that's an easy one. I found out in my neighborhood that I could make a dime a whole lot faster hustlin' on the streets rather than goin' to school or workin' a job. That's common sense on the street...make a dime or get a thrill as quick 'n easy as possible.

SOPHIA: Let's talk about Entitlement for a minute...do you re- member the story of God's children in Egypt?

KAI'RO: Yeah, they were slaves in Egypt for like 400 years.

SOPHIA: Yes, and God in His goodness delivered them from bond- age through miracles. He struck down the most powerful man in the world along with his army. Then He led His people with a cloud by day and a fire by night. Through amazing miracles He brought them food. But it wasn't long before the people started complain- ing and grumbling. They grew tired of the food He provided and felt that they were entitled to something better. They grew thirsty and started whining about the lack of water. When He gave them wa- ter, they didn't like the taste. Eventually they said that they'd settle for going back to slavery in Egypt rather than following God. They wanted Him to fix every problem and satisfy their every desire. But as soon as He did that, they just wanted more. This is an age old problem in the world. A lot of people grow up believing that some- one else should solve all their problems. They point at the govern- ment, their parents, the church, their schools, or their neighbors. If those people or organizations don't provide for them and solve all their issues, they whine and cry. Then, when those various or- ganizations step up to help, there is usually gratitude at first, but eventually most people begin to feel like they have a *right* to those things. The entitlement syndrome sets in and becomes something that cripples people. Again, this is an old problem that goes back to the beginning of time. It's is a problem that has spread all over the earth and is stuck in everyone's heart and life.

KAI'RO: You're right. You see this attitude everywhere in our country…in the hood *and* in the burbs. A lot of folks just think, "Hey, somebody else needs to fix or solve my problems."

SOPHIA: As I said to you earlier, the King's Word is true that you will reap what you sow. Those people who *chose* the booths *chose* to sow their LIFE into something that reaps no fruit. In fact it reaps death and meaninglessness in the end. Look throughout history to the beginning of time and you'll see that anyone who has chosen Blame, Entitlement, or Quick Fixes for their LIFE ends up in misery, pain, disappointment, and death. Wisdom says to *look* at the past *and* to watch those around you so you don't repeat their mistakes.

KAI'RO: Word.

SOPHIA: What about the Garden? What did you see there? Why did so few go?

KAI'RO: (laughing) That's a lot of work. Those folks were sweatin' and dirty. Someone comes up to me and says, "Hey, you can throw this ball and win a prize or you can bust your butt in the hot sun and plant some seeds, what'cha think I'm going to say?" But really… those people seemed to see their LIFE as more of an investment than a gamble. They were lookin' for some long term results.

SOPHIA: The Garden of Community and Responsibility. What do you think about that name?

KAI'RO: Well, RESPONSIBILITY is a key starting point to LIFE. Like you said everyone in the world grows up on a different part of the block so to speak. I mean some of us grew up in the hood and some grew up in the burbs. There's those that grew up in a mansion with food and some that grew up in a grass hut with nothin' but bugs. But the truth is we all received a LIFE from the King, and that's a gift. My life growin' up was nothin' to celebrate. I mean, I grew up broke and in a home with a lot of chaos and pain. There were folks miles down the road in the burbs that had it good…ya know…they had the nice house with the two-door garage. They went to good schools and had good families for the most part. I could see the difference between their lives and mine, and I used to use those differences as an excuse. But when I spent all my time blamin' people, blamin' my circumstances and whinin' for others to solve my problems, I was truly stuck. At some point I had to take RESPONSIBILITY for myself. For me, the starting point was taking RESPONSIBILITY for my own sin and mistakes. It meant making the RESPONSIBLE decision of giving my LIFE to the King and gettin' myself on the Heavenly Highway.

SOPHIA: Yes, that's the most important first decision.

KAI'RO: But it don't stop there. That's just where it all *begins*. Yeah, I had a sorry school system and a lousy home, but so do a lot of people all over the world. In fact there's a lot of folks who got it a lot worse. I never finished school, but I'm goin' to go back and get my GED. I can't allow all the drama and chaos in my life to be an excuse for not goin' forward. I gotta take some RESPONSIBIL-ITY for myself and by the King's grace start takin' some leaps forward in my LIFE. RESPONSIBILITY is an investment in yourself… an investment in excellence.

SOPHIA: And perhaps an investment in your own future…

KAI'RO: Yeah…responsibility is not just for *you*…it's about your future family, your kids, and maybe even your grandkids. I mean I've started to see the importance of hard work. I never had no man in the house who held down a job and showed me the impor-tance of providin' for his family. In fact, most of the guys who were in and out of my life provided for themselves by stealin' and hustlin'. That's how I learned to survive. But you know, the King said that those who steal should steal no longer, but should learn to work with their own hands. He even said that if somebody doesn't pro-vide for his own, particularly those in his own household, he has denied the faith and he's worse than an unbeliever. I don't ever want my kids to think it's normal for dads to dip out of the house, run the streets, get fired from every job, and shack up with other women. I don't want my son growin' up thinkin' that it's okay to take to the streets and take the easy road of crime to make ends meet. My dad passed nothin' on to me but a legacy of brokenness and abandonment. But that doesn't mean that I have to pass that same thing on to my kids. I'm gonna show 'em that a man leads by holdin' down a job, by comin' home each night, and by stayin' faithful to his wife. At some point somebody has to be responsible and step on the brakes and say, "Enough is enough." My family has been skidding down the road for as long as I can remember. Not no more…by the King's grace I'm goin' to put a stop to all that.

SOPHIA: (smiling) You are starting to see upside-down my child.

KAI'RO: Yeah…and COMMUNITY is crucial. We got some lousy and hurting neighborhoods. I grew up in one. But I gotta be honest…we got a lousy and hurting nation…shoot…we got a lousy and hurting world. Right now, most of us are too worried about ourselves and our own 'lil worlds. COMMUNITY is all about worryin' 'bout your neighbor and her needs and her hurts…it's 'bout teaming up with one another to make your streets livable again. It's about grabbin' a hammer and puttin' together the walls that have come down and jackin' up the foundation on places that have sunk in the mud.

SOPHIA: Yes! Yes! It's about loving your neighbor as much as yourself and about putting their needs before your own. Instead of demanding assistance for yourself, you give a helping hand to someone else. Instead of complaining about how you only have five pairs of shoes you give away four pairs to four people who have no shoes. You do this for your next door neighbor…but also for your neighbor on the other side of the world!

KAI'RO: It's all about changing the world one block at a time…

SOPHIA: One block at a time. *Exactly!* It's simple and you got it. I want you to understand two important facts in all of this. For one, the importance of investing your LIFE in RESPONSIBILITY and COMMUNITY are the King's principles. Notice the fruit to be reaped… HOPE, PURPOSE, MEANING, DAILY BREAD, PEACE, and DIRECTION. It's not necessarily an investment that's going to get you more money, but can you put a price tag on a life full of MEANING and HOPE? Who wouldn't want those things in their life? Amazingly, even someone who doesn't know or follow the King, but gives their life to RESPONSIBILITY and COMMUNITY will still reap the fruits of HOPE, PURPOSE, MEANING, DAILY BREAD, PEACE, and DIRECTION. They will obviously be in much smaller portions than one who knows and follows the King, but they are Kingdom principles that are good for followers and non-followers alike. The King's principles work regardless. This is an amazing truth. What is equally true is that even followers of the King will receive FLEETING PLEASURE, UNEARNED WAGES, SMALL COMFORT, MEANINGLESSNESS, BITTERNESS, and FRUSTRATION if they choose to invest their LIVES in BLAME, ENTITLEMENT and QUICK FIXES. The fruit of fleshly living and following the world's system will produce the same fruit, which is *nothing*…even in the lives of the King's followers. *Be aware of this!*

Secondly, notice that those who planted seeds produced more LIFE and fruit. You need to understand that those who have a relationship with the King receive eternal life, but the fruits that the trees yield are fruits for *today.* There is HOPE for today, MEANING for today, and PEACE for today! Following the King gives one LIFE forever, but also LIFE for each day. But at times the fruit is delayed. Those at the Garden received the fruit at different stages of their lives. Some immediately, and others well into their later years. But when the harvest was reaped , there was an abundance of fruit to share. Even with those who had none!

STORYTELLER: Sophia grabbed Kai'Ro's hand and led him gently out of the room and towards the exit.

SOPHIA: You have learned so much on this journey already.

KAI'RO: Back at the Interpreter's house I couldn't hardly understand a thing until he explained it all to me.

SOPHIA: Wisdom is a divine gift from the King. You must pray for it and He will give more of it to you. But you must also apply what knowledge you have gained to your life. Wisdom is putting Kingdom principles and knowledge to work in everyday life. The more you use it the more you'll sidestep the pain and frustration that you can easily bring on yourself. Yet, it is also a blessing to those who watch your life. As you walk on the path of Wisdom, others will notice how your life is different from theirs. You will avoid many of the holes that others fall into due to their own foolishness and lack of understanding.

KAI'RO: I hear what you're saying…but I don't know if anyone is really watchin' *my* life.

SOPHIA: (chuckling) Now that's a foolish thing for you to say, Kai'Ro. Everyone you meet is watching your life…some much more closely than others. What about your brother, Lil' One?

KAI'RO: (hanging his head) Yeah. He was watchin' and look where it got him…

SOPHIA: But is it over for him? Do you think he is done watching and learning from you his big brother? What about some of your old friends?

KAI'RO: I'm tryin' to get away from those bad memories and influences! I wouldn't mind gettin' out of the hood for good. You know… maybe get me a good job and a place to live in a nice neighborhood that doesn't have all the drama and nonsense.

SOPHIA: Kai'Ro, you must continue to see with an upside-down view. How many people have left the hood, left areas of decay and areas of pain simply to make their own life easier? Did not the King leave a place of peace and security for a place of danger and death? He left a platinum throne in heaven and He chose to be born in a wooden box full of animal spit and straw. He gave up streets of gold to walk the dusty and stinking roads of this world. The King left a place where He ruled over angels for a place where mere men would show Him no respect, beat Him bloody, and curse Him. Finally, they would kill Him.

KAI'RO: Yeah, you're right. I guess I just don't know if that's what I'm called to do…

SOPHIA: 'Calling' is a curious thing. It's not *wrong* to live in the suburbs or in a community of peace, but hardly anyone ever claims that they're 'called' to be in such a community. Why? Because to make such a decision is relatively easy. No one will second guess them. Yet, don't you think that people should consider their calling no matter where they live? Just because a decision makes sense doesn't necessarily mean it's the right decision. What I'm talking to you about right now, Kai'Ro, is not necessarily Wisdom…although Wisdom is part of such a decision. What I'm talking to you about now is Compassion. That is a choice to give up your LIFE and spend it on those who do not have life in them. It's the sacrificial step of following the King into a place where no one else would willingly go because they have fear, insecurity, and doubt. You can't get past sacrifice, Kai'Ro. Not if you really want to follow Him. Too many people cling to the comforts of this life instead. They are unwilling to give up the things that are dear to them—the material possessions, the lusts of the eye, and greed for wealth become distractions that prevent them from following after the King. These folks give up their very soul in an attempt to gain this world around them. But can you put a price tag on your *soul*?

KAI'RO: I hear what you're sayin', but I'm also worried that my old crowd will drag me down again. There's too much temptation and bad memories back in the City of Doom!

SOPHIA: This is true. Yet, you have already come so far. You have grown in Wisdom. With the King's Word in your heart, and His Wisdom in your mind, He will guide you in regards to whom you should help and from whom you should run. It is true that there are some old friends that it would be better for you to run from. But there are also people there who need your help and they need to see a life like yours to give them hope. Remember this: there are always others that the King has raised up to go on this journey with you. You don't have to go at it alone. You are *not* alone.

STORYTELLER: Kai'Ro stared hard at Sophia. He put both of his hands on his head and sighed.

KAI'RO: I will pray about what you are saying to me.

SOPHIA: (smiling) That is a good place to start. I am with you always, son.

STORYTELLER: There was a bright flash that caused Kai'Ro to cover his eyes. When he put his arms down again, Sophia and the Circus of Wisdom were gone. He was alone on the Heavenly Highway, and there were decisions he had to make.

CHAPTER SIXTEEN:
BROKEN &
THE HARVEST

STORYTELLER: Kai'Ro spun himself slowly in a circle looking at the road behind him and the road ahead. He had come so far, and now he did not know exactly where to go.

KAI'RO: (to himself) What should I do? King, I cry out to you for direction. Fill my heart with your heart and my mind with your mind so that I might better know what I've got to do.

STORYTELLER: As if in answer to his prayer, a young lady came walking towards him down the road. She was very thin and very pretty. Her head was bowed low and she was staring at the ground as she walked. Her arms were wrapped around her body as if she were trying to stay warm. As she drew closer, Kai'Ro could see that she was crying. Then, to his surprise he recognized her!

KAI'RO: Broken? Is that you, girl?

STORYTELLER: Broken looked up, and when she saw Kai'Ro she smiled a little bit.

BROKEN: Kai'Ro? I can't believe it. I haven't seen you in the longest.

KAI'RO: Yeah. This is so crazy. What'cha doin'?

STORYTELLER: Broken looked back at the ground.

BROKEN: Nothin' for real. I'm just out walkin'.

KAI'RO: Didn't you graduate not too long ago?

BROKEN: (smiling) Top of the class.

KAI'RO: Girl, that's awesome. So you gotta be goin' to college, right? I mean if anyone from our class could do it, it's you.

BROKEN: Yeah, see that's the thing...I ain't got no money to go to college.

KAI'RO: No money? Didn't you apply for scholarships? Top of the class and you didn't get no scholarships or nothin'?

BROKEN: I couldn't get my mama to fill out anything, Kai'Ro . (Crying again). She got back on the drugs again and me and my 'lil sister had to spend all kinds of time just tryin' to keep her from literally killin' herself. It was like all I could do just to care for her and then try and study to pass my tests. We had the power cut off at the house and even went for almost two weeks with no food. Mama didn't reapply for food stamps. She was too strung out. Finally a pastor got some folks from the church to straighten stuff out for us.

KAI'RO: But there was no way for you get some help with college?

BROKEN: My mom came to graduation, ya know? She was all proud 'cause I was the first person to graduate from high school in my whole family's history. It was a big thing to me, and I was so proud of myself. I felt like I did somethin' honorable for my whole family. Well, about two days after graduation I was tryin' to get my mama to fill out some financial paperwork for me. I think I would have qualified for the moon. My mama just put the pen down and pushed the paperwork away. Do you know what she said to me, Kai'Ro…?

STORYTELLER: She burst into tears and had a really tough time pulling herself together.

BROKEN: She told me that the best thing I could do for myself and my future was to get pregnant and get on that Section 8. Can you believe that?

KAI'RO: What? Your mom told you to do that? That's crazy! I'm so sorry she said that to you. I can't believe it. You didn't listen to that nonsense did you?

BROKEN: I was crushed. I was mad. I ran outta the house and disappeared for like two weeks or somethin'. I guess I was just runnin' the streets. I had a friend round the way…a boy named No-Good, and so I hung out at his place.

STORYTELLER: Kai'Ro shook his head and then rubbed his hands down his face.

BROKEN: I couldn't believe my mama would say somethin' so ugly to me…particularly after me and my sister had done so much for her. Well, I finally went home and found out more bad news. The deadline for all those scholarships and financial aid had passed. I wouldn't get a dime. Plus, my mama was so strung out on drugs again she couldn't hardly talk to me. Then I found out the hardest news of all, Kai'Ro…

STORYTELLER: Kai'Ro looked at her and waited for her to speak.

BROKEN: (sniffing) I found out I was pregnant…

STORYTELLER: Broken fell forward and would have collapsed to the ground but Kai'Ro rushed forward and caught her. He held her close while she bawled her eyes out on his chest. I could see tears rolling down his face as well as he looked up to heaven. Along the cracked Highway he held her for a long time as she sobbed. Finally, Kai'Ro spoke.

KAI'RO: So, what'cha goin' to do now?

BROKEN: What'cha think? I'm goin' to be a mama now and I am goin' to go get on that Section 8. My mama's words came true. Who knew I was goin' to do the exact thing she said?

KAI'RO: So that's it? You're just tossin' all those college dreams in the trash, girl? You got no hope now?

BROKEN: What hope *is* there?

STORYTELLER: Broken wrestled free from Kai'Ro's hug and glared at him.

BROKEN: There ain't no hope for me, and there ain't no hope for the City of Doom neither. You know the place too. It's a hellhole and nobody gets out…nobody goes anywhere. It's like a city for the dead. Don't talk about hope, like it's somethin' you can just go buy at the store and it can solve all ya problems. That ain't how it works, Kai'Ro!

STORYTELLER: Kai'Ro looked a bit shocked at her anger, and seemed lost for words. Then I saw a fire emerge in his eyes and he put a strong hand on her shoulder.

KAI'RO: You're right! Hope don't grow on trees. But hope ain't somethin' you can't find. Hope is real. And I've got hope. Look at me, girl! Right now I'm a high school dropout with no job and no where to live. I broke up with my girlfriend, Evangeline. My friends all left me when I needed them the most. And even before all that I was just someone who fell into the cracks and into the dark spaces in the ground. I coulda stayed there, but I found hope. Yeah, I found it! I'm not talkin' about no weak hope—the kind of weak hope you feel when you get a paycheck or make an 'A' on a test. I'm talkin' 'bout a hope that's so deep and so real and so strong that I feel like I'm goin' to burst! I found that hope when I was the most hopeless. I was locked up like an animal for crimes I had committed. Weighed down by my own guilt and shame, I just wanted to die. I had been in and out of jail since I was a shortie, and knew almost every cop in town by name. I'd done a lot of bad things…some that I will never repeat because they're too bad and too embarrassin' to talk about. It was in that stinkin' jail, in a cell too small for a mouse let alone a man, that I found hope. Through the bars of my cell a Preacher man came. He introduced me to hope for the first time when he introduced me to a blameless and powerful King who was willin' to take all my shame and make it His shame. This perfect King was willin' to take all my guilt and make it His guilt. He was even willin' to take all my failures, shortcuts, goof-ups, screw-ups, and every absurd thing I'd done and take blame for all of it for me. That sounded good to me. I mean, I was a criminal, and this King was apparently goin' to take my rap sheet and take the blame for it all. But then this guy told me somethin' that shocked me. He told me that according to the Creator of the world, my rap sheet deserved the death penalty. In fact he said that everyone has a rap sheet and everyone deserves the death penalty because that rap sheet offends a holy and perfect Creator. But he said this blameless King was not goin' to let me die for those things. This King volunteered to die *himself* for all those things. In fact, when He turned himself in, they beat Him with their fists and with whips until nobody could recognize Him no more. Then, they stretched Him out on this big ole cross and pounded nine-inch spikes through His wrists and feet. All for *me.* The King hung up there for hours until He died. And He did this for me, and for *you*, Broken.

BROKEN: I don't know…

KAI'RO: Look, hopelessness is what sets in on ya when ya get to the point where all your struggles, failures, guilt, and circumstances become like a stain on your soul that you can't get out no matter how hard you try. I mean, that's how I was in that jail. I wanted to die at that point 'cause I was weighed down by everything I'd done—all the lies I'd told, stuff I'd stole, all the people I'd hurt, and all the shame that went with those things. Those things were a part of who I was, and at that time I felt like there was no way I'd ever be able to get rid of 'em or get separated from 'em. You're in that place now. Be honest with yourself, you made a mistake. In fact, you made a *bad* mistake, but that doesn't mean it's all over for ya now. That doesn't mean that all hope is lost. This King that I follow promises that He'll work all things out for our good…even our shame and mistakes! Now, I don't know exactly how He's gonna do that for you, but I believe He will if you're willin' to give your life and all that's in it to Him.

STORYTELLER: Broken stared at Kai'Ro. In her eyes I could see a deep longing for truth.

BROKEN: Word made it back to the City that you had gotten religious. A lot of people made fun of you and said it was just a matter of time before you came back to your old ways and your old friends. Fact is, I've had a lot of friends get religious on me before. And true enough, they ended up goin' back to their old ways and usually ended up goin' into stuff a lot worse. But you, you don't got no religion, Kai'Ro. It's like you gotta *relationship* with this King you've been talkin' about. You talk about Him as if He's your best friend or somethin'.

KAI'RO: He is.

BROKEN: I've never met nobody like you before. Back when you was at the City of Doom you were so strong, but you were angry and hard. You still look strong, but it's like, I don't know. It's like you have a whole new kinda strong. I can see it in your eyes… Thank you for talkin' with me, Kai'Ro. You've lifted me up.

KAI'RO: So what'cha goin' to do now?

BROKEN: Well, I know what I'm *not* goin' to do.

KAI'RO: What's that?

BROKEN: I'm not goin' to give up. I'm not goin' on that Section 8 like my mama said I should.

KAI'RO: Yeah?

BROKEN: (smiling) Yeah!

KAI'RO: What about what I said 'bout the King?

BROKEN: Don't know yet. You gave me a lot to think about. I mean…everythin' you said hit me somewhere deep. I heard everything you said. I'm not sure I'm ready to give my life to no King just yet…but I'd sure like to have the same peace and strength I see in your face right now. If that's the only way to get it…well, then I might just give my life to Him.

KAI'RO: Sometimes that decision takes time. But when you give your life to the King, He gives you His life in return. That's the biggest blessin'. Any peace, joy, hope, love, or life you see in my life is 'cause He's livin' in me now. That's the biggest and best part about it. I'll pray for you, Broken. I'll pray that you find your life in His because you'll never be the same. I promise.

BROKEN: Thanks again, Kai'Ro. I hope to see you again. The City of Doom could use a man like you around. (Chuckling) That armor you got on is goin' to cause a few people to crack…but I think it's cool. I think you'd do a whole lot a good.

STORYTELLER: The two hugged. Broken thanked him one more time and then turned back in the direction from which she had come. Kai'Ro watched her until she disappeared over the hill.

KAI'RO: (sighing and looking towards the sky) Okay, King, I think I'm gettin' the message. You want me to go back to my old stompin' grounds. I'll be honest…I don't feel like it at all. But you said in your Word that the folks who bring your Good News to the poor and to the lost have "beautiful feet." Someone brought beautiful feet to me in that jail cell a long time ago. I'd be a thief and sellout if I didn't do the same for somebody else.

STORYTELLER: Kai'Ro paced back and forth for a while with his face pointed towards the heavens. His lips were moving, but in my dream I could not hear what he was saying. Then he stopped and started walking back towards the City of his birth. He walked on for quite some time. His face was hard like flint, but in his eyes was a softness and a love and a fire. The sun was high in the sky and beating down on him. Ahead was a tall shade tree. He walked over to it and leaned against it, enjoying the shade. To his left was a crumbled brick wall. Graffitied on the side of the wall was the phrase, "The harvest is plentiful, but the workers are few…" Kai'Ro smiled. After waiting for a period of time, he set off again until he came to a Crossroads. There was a sign leading to the City of Doom and another sign that went to a city called Tarshish.

KAI'RO: Naw, I ain't goin' to be like Jonah and set off somewhere else…even though I don't feel like goin' back. The King told Jonah to go to a place and part of him was afraid and part of him hated those people. So, he disobeyed the King and ended up in a fish's belly for like three days. There's part of *me* that's afraid, and I'll be honest, there's a part of me that *hates* a lot of those people back there at the City of Doom. But there ain't no way I want to end up no belly of a fish. So I'm goin', O King! I'm goin'!

STORYTELLER: Kai'Ro walked and walked and walked. His mind was imagining all kinds of things. Sometimes his face got tense from fear. Other times, he smiled. After a great while he made it back into the open countryside again. There were large green trees, rolling hills, and fresh air. He stopped from time to time to soak it all up. He breathed in the beauty. But before long he could see the dense smog in the distance. There was a reddish black cloud just beyond the horizon. He squinted his eyes, and he could see the shadows of tall buildings. He exhaled a deep breath.

KAI'RO: The City of Doom. A home for the lost and dyin'. A place where the streets are drenched with blood and the homes are full of horror. It's a city of killers, thieves, and pimps. It's a place where women are nothin' more than property. Children are forgotten with the trash. I'm comin' back to bring you Good News. I'm returnin' to give you some hope and point you towards Life. You may be the place where I was born, but you ain't my home no more. My home is in Heaven, and my ruler is a King. Your 'ole boy, Kai'Ro, is comin' back. But I ain't the same, and I pray you'll be ready. You may hear me or ya may hate me. Ya may hug me or ya may hit me. Ya might care for me, or ya might kill me. But it don't matter 'cause I love ya and I want to introduce you to the One who can save ya. The King has sent me back…so here I come!

STORYTELLER: Suddenly, Kai'Ro took off in a sprint. He shot off down the old dirt road like lightning, kicking up a cloud of dust as he went. He stopped when he came to the old hedges just outside the City. He parted the bushes with his hands, crawled inside, and disappeared from my sight. Then, I awoke.